Desahogo: The Undrowning

Carmen Mojica

Desahogo: The Undrowning
Copyright © 2024 Carmen Mojica

All rights reserved. No part of this publication may be reproduced, distributed, or transmitted in any form or by any means, without written authorization by the author, except in the case of brief quotations embodied in critical reviews and certain other noncommercial uses permitted by copyright law.

Cover design:
Brandon Chacon

Editors:
Amanda Alcántara
Nicole Lawrence

Author cover photo:
Jonathan Rojas

ISBN-13: 979-8-218-40918-0

Desahogar is one of my favorite words in Spanish. It translates to vent, but if you break it down the literal translation, it means to undrown. As if letting go of the burden and secrets you are holding onto will be the thing to save you from drowning. What a beautiful image.
- Nia Ita Thomas

Dedication

To all the survivors.

Thank You

Elisabet Velasquez, and her fiancé Johnathan Rojas, for being my photography team. Brandon Chacon, for the cover design, the revisions and attention to detail.

Andre Lee Muniz, for granting me the greatest gift in my life of being a mother.

To Gabbie and J Warren: the most important therapists I've ever had.

Melissa Smith-Tourville, for saving my life and stepping into a gap that has always been missing in my life.

Amanda Alcantara, for cheering me on this project and for all the years of friendship and creativity.

Nicole Lawrence, for the hours we spent talking about this book, the editing, and the push to finish this.

Anastasia Libovich and Ashley Colon, for being the best sister-friends I could ask for.

All the women in my life, past and present, who have contributed to my healing journey.

Content Warning:
This literary work is explicit in themes of sexuality, sexual violence & assault, mental health, suicide, and suicide ideation. There is a graphic description of sexual assault.

All That Glitters

Vanity was his favorite sin. In women, to be precise.

Hades saw her standing off to the side in a frilly dress. Much too old to be dressed up like a doll, Persephone peeked from behind a column at everyone around her. She was required to be there but didn't seem to be welcomed to the gathering. It was another stuffy soirée in Hera's sitting room. They always had a high-end tea every week and he was amused at the pretense and forced smiles.

Hades had pecan-colored skin. He wore a black fedora over his balding head and had dark brown eyes that seemed slightly sunken in. Hades was slender and muscular, his biceps rippling whenever he flexed or balled his hands into a fist. The rest of his attire was black: a black trench coat with the sleeves cut off, black slacks, and black combat boots. A cigar was sometimes lit in his mouth. He was attractive enough but his aura was intense.

He lived in a world of long faces and silence. This was much more entertaining than the dead and forgotten. Hera sat on her rose-gold throne looking stunning. Her high cheekbones were accentuated with bronze highlight, sharp severe contour to match the kohl black eye makeup heavily lining her eyes. The blackness was only rivaled by the jet-black hair pulling her eyes up at her temples into a neat perfect bun. She wore silk and satin robes in jewel colors. Her long black stiletto nails were flawless; she impatiently tapped them on her table as she watched her sister goddess subjects milling around.

Hera had eyes like a hawk. She inspected and surveyed every inch of her room for imperfections. The molding needed dusting, a fly was buzzing about undetected by nearly everyone, the tea was not steeped long enough and the food needed more salt. She sighed in annoyance as she took mental notes for her berating of her chambermaids later.

"The Prosecco," she ordered from a shadow standing beside her.

"We've not yet started the tea…"
"That's not what I asked, imbecile. Get me my drink," Hera growled through gritted teeth.
The shadow scurried away to avoid disaster. The Queen of Olympus was already in a rotten mood. This is to say, the queen was always in varying levels of foul and disgust.

Hades chuckled staring at his oldest sister. What a pathetic joke of a queen. Hera couldn't even get the attention of Zeus on her own - Aphrodite would never let her live down the fact that her girdle was the reason. She gave her king her heart and he repaid her in dirty drawers and lingering perfume that smelled like roses. Zeus gathered roses for her once. For far too long, Hera would have fresh roses all over her powder room. She'd fashion crowns of them and inhale the scent deeply, intoxicating herself with the idea of his love.

Now she knew that it was the scent of a new conquest. The aroma would fill the hallway when the doors of his bedroom chamber would fly open in the days of his younger years. The palace would endure the wrath of Hera's rage: she routinely took shears to the curtains and the tapestries, ripped open all his pillows and mattress, and set fire to his robes.

Everyone knew Zeus was a womanizer. He learned from his forefathers how to crush women up for his pleasure only. Los ojos se le llenaron de mujeres de la tierra. It kept him and his trysts out of the palace and out of Hera's immediate sight.

Hera could do nothing about it but rage and take it out on the sluts and whores who dared be tempted by her husband. The royal court was full of open secrets and bastard children who knew a distant father and virgin mothers. Zeus, after all, was untouchable. No crime or accusation could stick to him nor any mortal wound that could injure him. So the women paid for his indiscretions.

The worst for Hera seemed to be Demeter. Why did Zeus ever want that ugly bitch? The one who never bothered with elegance and decorum? La fucking loca, of all people.

Crazy bitches fuck with abandon.

Demeter's lips were a thin pressed line crooked on her face. Her nose was wide and round, and her cheeks were high but full, as though she retained the buccal fat Hera had removed for safekeeping. The concealer under her eyes was no match for the darkness there. Demeter had done everything to hide beneath the mask she painted on. Somehow, the time she spent getting ready was never enough to look como la gente. Her thin straw-like hair was disheveled, as though she had fought it with a brush and lost. Wrinkled and stained, her camel-colored dress at least was her size however informal it was. Did she even fucking try to look good? Hera had half a mind to send her away to the stables where she belonged. Instead, Hera cherished that she would always look stunning next to this waste of space.

And how dare she have a gorgeous daughter? How she hated Persephone. This little dark-skinned girl scorched by Helios should have been uglier than Hera had been. She had made sure of it by ordering it.

But no.

Hades went back to lay eyes on Persephone. She was on the precipice of womanhood, her budding curves being contained in the way her mother dressed her. Persephone's skin was a unique shade of mahogany, with tight black curls rebelling against all and every attempt to be tamed. He had plans for that little girl. There had been a prophecy told to him that a daughter of Zeus would be the one to overthrow the reign of the patriarchy on Earth. It had to be this little delicious morsel of neglected sunshine. He slowly approached her, moving in the shadows to avoid Demeter's eyes.

He saw Persephone notice him, fear evident in her eyes. He had a secret weapon. Flashing his dazzling smile at her, he softened his aura and eased the evil that oozed out of him. A cold chill went up her spine as he got close enough to feel his hot breath on her neck.

"You look very pretty today."
Persephone looked down, her cheeks getting hot. No one ever complimented her. She

wanted to smile but had been taught to be scared of Hades. She said nothing. Hades reached into his pocket and pulled out a tarot card deck.

"It's your birthday today, isn't it?" he mused. Persephone's eyes widened. No one remembered her birthday. Ever.
"Ye-ye-yes," she stammered, trying not to smile too hard.

"Happy birthday, Persephone. Please accept this gift from me," Hades said. *Why would anyone be afraid of him?* she thought to herself. He was the only one who ever paid attention to her. And this gesture was enough to have her hooked. It would take much longer for that tiny seed to blossom into something only Hades could cultivate - beautiful but deadly.

The Tension Between Me and My Poetry

My poetry is the best sex partner
I've ever had.
I write to cum to an understanding of my
identity, to have a mind-blowing orgasm that
sends all types of metaphors and similes up
and down my spine and my legs go weak
with the way poetry penetrates profusely into
me making mockeries of minuscule men who
might never know what it's like to go deep.
Call me oversexed but the world as I view it
is an orgy and we're all getting fucked;
I just chose to do my poetry on the side. I'm
tired of faking it - my entire existence that is.

Mochanvas

Dip the paintbrush ever so slowly into the
water
Watch crayon-like rectangles become liquid
Become part of the canvas
Start with just one touch of the brush to
fresco, fingertips pressed gently to soften the
deafening silent impact of a concept onto a
prophesied masterpiece

I trace shadows that define depth and
enhance clarity, wishing my fingers were as
quick as my thoughts
Losing myself in the abyss of one stroke, two
strokes
I blend the colors I think in on my palette
And speak in hues I dream in, they leave my
fingertips like blown-away eyelashes, like
mosaics of metaphors I carefully construct to
convey a thousand words in one instant
I find I don't speak much when my body is
pressed up against canvas, barely touching
each other
Wooden brush is the bridge between woman
and creation
I can't tell what is the art because as I create it,
I become it

My skin morphs into a workspace
Holding the skin smoothly, mocha-colored
canvas
Create art

Imitate life
Paint on me
Slide fingertips that glide across miles of
seamless skin
Follow the contour

Observe shadow
Make goosebumps form a landscape for
sunsets only painted after observing one from
rooftops overlooking 'hoods and capturing
that feeling
Dip fingers into the water
Pick a new color.
Paint a new direction.
A different stroke
Etched marks of permanence,
I want to be timeless like the Sistine Chapel
Beautifully soulful as Pieta
Surreal like a Dali painting
I channel life into these hands and continue
the tradition
Of art imitating life imitating art

Demeter, La Loca

She was never quite the same after her father swallowed her. After Zeus rescued them, it was said that Demeter was mute for seven years. There was always something off about her.

When she did finally speak, she was boisterous and lewd. Anything that came to her mind was blurted out without thought. She never covered her mouth when she laughed loudly, cackling from her belly always.

Demeter used to be a stick of a woman. She'd been cast to the earth after Hera learned of Zeus lying with her. Rumor has it that Demeter had shamelessly laid in his bed awaiting him and Zeus could care less who it was as long as it was that royal Olympian pussy. Other accounts point to Zeus finding Demeter in the fields as she was gently encouraging the wheat and grains to grow for her people. For some reason, the wheat germ that year was bitter from the tears she shed the entirety of the pregnancy that resulted from it.

A mind on the edge was fractured nonetheless after the encounter, and it wasn't clear if it was her natural disposition to be unhinged or if she was pushed to her breaking point. Year after year, the harvest became more and more unpredictable, much like Demeter's moods. She was at times overflowing with creative energy, nurturing the earth and fostering abundant growth. Other times, Demeter was impulsive and erratic, causing sudden shifts in the weather patterns. The humans tried to appease her constantly with sacrifices and festivals.

In the midst of spring, Demeter would sweep across the land like a whirlwind. The once-dormant fields burst to life with an explosion of color and fragrance. She would dance through the meadows, her laughter echoing across the countryside.

Flowers bloomed effortlessly as she moved and frolicked, their petals unfurling eagerly to greet the warm sunlight. With a wave of her hand, she would command the clouds to part, allowing the sun to shine its golden rays upon the earth below. The air filled with the scent of freshly turned soil and the promise of abundance. The humans watched in awe as their crops sprung from the ground, maturing at an unprecedented rate.

Just as suddenly, she would plummet into profound despair. The days became shorter and Demeter would withdraw into herself, neglecting her duties and allowing the earth

to wither and die. Her sorrow permeated the land, leading to famine and desolation.
Her once light and fanciful feet dragged heavy on the ground. Demeter would wander through the barren fields with tears streaming down her face.

The earth would lie cold, a lifeless wasteland. Leafless trees stood in the icy landscape, and the air was heavy with the weight of grief. A chilling silence hung over the land. The humans watched helplessly as their crops wilt and die, the harsh winter taking its toll on the land. They would choose between nourishing themselves and sacrificing the cows that remained in hopes that Demeter would return with plentiful crops in the next season.

She always woke up in a frenzy; so much so that Persephone learned to never wake her mother up despite the 12 hours she'd appear lifeless in her bed. It is as though Demeter never grew out of the startle response.

Demeter loved her daughter. She did. She just never learned to be a mother. Rhea fed them all to Cronus because he was afraid to be overthrown, but never recovered from the trauma. Demeter never fed Persephone to anyone physically. She was proud of that. Keeping her daughter sheltered and out of sight was the best she could do.

As Persephone got older, hiding was no longer enough. The closer she got to the age that Demeter had her, the more Persephone found her mother unavailable. That is to say, her mother kept her clean and dressed but left so much to be desired.

Eventually, Demeter's pain would seep out of her and damage the little bit of relationship they had. Once, Persephone was afraid of her mother's rage and lied about where she had been and Demeter called her a liar. Over and over again. She would accuse Persephone of being a fast little girl when she'd see her talking to any of the male gods. Once she called her a prostitute when she was sitting on Poseidon's lap as a little girl and chastised her for trying to seduce him. Another time, she slapped Persephone when there were rumors about her and Adonis. And so, this is how Demeter lost her long before she was stolen away.

Summer of Art

In the breeze that introduces summer to the
stage of the seasons as they ripple through
this earth
I danced with my skirt bunched up in my fist,
talking philosophies on life into the folds of
our eyes the way artists sometimes do

We said that night, we would never sacrifice
the love at the expense of having no reason to
rise from beds too tempting and too safe to
leave otherwise

Observe shape
As clearly as the sun defies night on the
longest day of the year, the seemingly
intricate design has a method to it
She shed tears for him that morning after, as
we realized night could not shroud us in
mystery for much longer

We learn shapes of hearts don't determine
their kindness or perseverance
Everything is illuminated when we feel alive
Countless peace pipes shared between sisters,
between lovers, we light lighters in dark
spaces so they never forget the day.
You wake up inches from my face so
I don't forget what a human body can feel
like inside me

The shape of your eyes intrigues me to stare
The same way sculptors and painters do
when we create art together

Observe shape, contour
Make sure the lighting is right
And remember our lives are made up of lines

An artist said that to his student once
He wanted her to remember curves are just
transformed lines

Every pen stroke, measure it. Savor every
single second of this moment before it dries.
Every single slight touch of my fingers in
your clay-like skin reminds me that I cannot
change your composition, but my imprint is
still noted, yet transient

Bending me like a beam of light, a new
dimension created in the blankness of time
and space

The lighting on the pattern of your infinite
skin was perfect that night, only but slightly
accentuating the highlights of your jaw line,
and the ridge right under your eye that
becomes the predecessor to your cheekbone

I notice the shadows the light casts upon you
And it is then that it becomes clear to me the
mystique of dark and light
I could imagine this

And every brush stroke
Study the image before your paintbrush
touches the canvas
Stare
No
Really reach your gaze into the blankness of
what you thought tomorrow was, and realize
what it can become

The untapped potential of your very
existence depends on this portrait of what we
think we see and what is really there

Observe space
Hold out your pencil, out in the air to
measure the distance of what it

It is possible to recreate dimensions
When I find myself translating your body
into a speaking pattern my soul understands
Fundamentally listening to every syllable we
breathe into the air when we speak in circles
we've drawn around each other

These days I feel my heart pulsing in my ear
reminding me to listen to each passion I was
born with inside
And I find the sketches of conversation
created on rooftops as the sun and moon
were juxtaposed in perfect balance
The same way one side of a scale gazes at the
other

It's all about the details, he told me one night
as we walked to the train station aware of the
design we exist in
And I came home one night, held her face in
my hands to study the colors of her eyes
They are green, they are blue, they are the
ocean
Spokes of colors like wheels of vision that
caress her pupils
I missed them

I've refused to see the rainbows hidden in
your sky, tucked away in your smiles
Until you told me to look at you that
afternoon
And it was then I saw
That with eyes wide open the fleeting realities
crossing my line of vision are not as two-
dimensional as once perceived

Zeus, The Head Rapist

His father Cronus ate his siblings alive. Zeus
was told this later while he was sequestered
on the island of Crete and as a little boy, had
nightmares of a monster eating children alive.

Cronus castrated Uranus, became the ruler of
the universe, and married his sister Rhea. She
had six children, Zeus, his elder sisters, and
elder brothers: Hestia, Demeter, Poseidon,
Hera, and Hades. As one could imagine,
Cronus was not just power-hungry but a
paranoid sick fuck. He swallowed each child
as soon as they were born. Before he castrated
Uranus, his father told him that Cronus
would meet the same fate and be overthrown
too by one of his children.
Rhea hated Cronus. What else would a
mother feel watching her terrible husband
swallow her children?

Her pleas were discarded the same way
Cronus shoved her hard into the wall, out of
the way, as she covered her babies with her
body. Grief-stricken five times, she sought out
the counsel of her mother Gaia. She fled to
the island of Crete to birth Zeus. The boy was
raised by his grandmother and Cronus was
given a swaddled stone to swallow.
Cronus hadn't noticed. He never has. If we're
being honest, one can see where Zeus got his

hubris. Anything smaller than them was insignificant.

Zeus grew rapidly into a dashing young man. He knew no mother or father and thus became self-important. He forgot those nightmares as a child and how he cried himself to sleep wanting someone to hold him. The nymphs and Gaia kept him alive but other than that, he was raised by the world of men around him.

He was attractive enough but had no game. But he was strong and charming. Women to him were a dime a dozen and he could never have enough.

Eventually, he was told of his fate to overthrow Cronus and got high off the thought of being omnipotent. But his hands alone would not suffice. He ordered his grandmother to give Cronus an emetic, which made his father vomit out his siblings. Next, he woke up the Cyclops who gifted him the thunderbolt in gratitude. And so began the war of the Gods and the Titans.

As the story goes, the Titans were defeated and locked in the Underworld. Zeus assumed the throne on Mount Olympus, and as the supreme patriarch, focused on the one thing he wanted: pussy. Olympian pussy first, of course.

Hera was his second wife after Thetis. He was never into his sister like that until Aphrodite lent her the girdle. Poor Hera thought that was enough to keep the ravenous beast at bay. And for a while, he did court her and love her the way her father should have. Zeus didn't swallow her; admittedly he was never very good at cunnilingus and devouring people whole never appealed to him. But her heart was his favorite dessert.

The stories of his conquest were innumerable.

Correction.

The countless women and goddesses he raped were seen as inconsequential to him. He wanted whatever the fuck he wanted and that was that. And the men of the earth followed suit.

His other wife was Metis, the goddess of good counsel. Not that Zeus ever listened to her. Upon getting her pregnant, he feared being overthrown. He swallowed Metis to prevent the birth but from his head, Athena sprung out fully grown and ready for war. Ms. Athena was the goddess of wisdom and warfare. She was self-important and couldn't stand being treated like a woman, challenged by a man, or disrespected.

It is important to note that he fucked Metis to spite Hera for conceiving asexually and giving birth to Hephaestus, the god of the forge and metallurgy. Zeus, the almighty, couldn't bear the fact that this son of his was lame. He went on and slept with the goddess of justice, divine order, and law, Themis, and begot the Hours. He went on and fucked Mnemosyne nine times and had the Muses, then turned her into a goddamn river in the Underworld. At least she'd always remember that asshole.

Then there was Leto. She was minding her business, a quietly beautiful woman. Leto accidentally caught Zeus' wandering eyes and he fucked her. It must be also said that this dude has super sperm and gets everyone pregnant. He got her pregnant with the wonder twins, Apollo (sometimes a piece of shit god) and Artemis (a skilled huntress who was kind but aloof). Hera got tight and ordered all the lands to turn Leto away, denying her shelter and somewhere to give birth. She gave birth on a piece of land that was in the gray area of Hera's decree. Hera was a bitch about it though and made Leto labor for days before they gave birth.

Then there was Io, Hera's priestess. Zeus saw how beautiful Io was and pursued her, then slept with her. Then hid this from Hera and turned Io into a heifer.

Semele was the mother of Dionysus, the god of wine and festivity. Zeus seduced her and got Semele pregnant with his incredibly precise sperm. Hera went after her but had some fun in the process. She disguised herself as an old midwife and began talking shit about Zeus to Semele. Hera told her that her lover wasn't a god and that Semele should ask to see him in his full form. Zeus, in one of the few instances of remorse and reluctance, had to show her himself, and the poor woman was burned to a crisp. Zeus took the baby and put the child in his thigh, and thus Dionysus was born. Very weird.

Golden showers, anyone? Zeus was the first one. He transformed himself into a shower of gold and impregnated Danae by pouring all over her because he just couldn't help himself.

He raped Europa, a teen girl, while she was minding her damn business by turning into a bull, luring her on his back, and carrying her away from her friends. They named a whole damn continent after the poor girl.

Ganymede was barely a footnote. He was taken to the palace of the gods to live alongside them as an immortal and serve as Zeus's cupbearer and lover. Though, with his young age, it was highly unlikely that he had a choice in any of this.

There are several other victims but the point is, Zeus wasn't just a piece of shit power-hungry asshole -- he was the head rapist in charge.

Inspired

Slowly, with a measured hand
he glides his brush on the infinite canvas
His paint, a trail of
lavenders and periwinkle blues
a replica of the early summer sky he saw in
the paintings on the walls of her thighs

He tinted the horizon hues of pinks and reds
like the blush of her insides
and the warmth of her pursed scarlet lips,
leaving an imprint on napkin to remind him
of the original sin

As the stars twinkle, her eyes glowed a
brilliant light; he poked holes in them
pressed them into the darkness
so he could find his way into the crevice
of her clavicles and the twilight of her breasts

Morning's first lights
before the sun stopped by again
were awoken by her throaty songs
as he gently searched between her legs
for the next stroke of inspiration

<u>Your Influence</u>

My body is different after you've been in it;
Hips wider from accommodating yours
grinding into them
Everything, more fluid.
*You warmed my blood; it circulates with more
purpose*
Pelvis moving to muscle memory of -
Gyrating, sliding rhythmically with the rest
of my serpentine body
Beneath you, facing you
A live wire thrashing some nights
A water hose flagellating
My body is a conduit for electric lightning
storms brewing between us;
I study myself naked in the mirror as though
you left a map on it.
There are places you left relics buried in
Your echo reverberates in the caves of my
crevices
It is a new land I find myself exploring each
dawning day
It is ephemeral, this thing you've known.

Adonis and Persephone

He was a beautiful young boy. Aphrodite fancied him, especially after the death of his wretched mother. Adonis was the son of Myrrha, a dirty whore who lusted for her father, the king of Cyprus. He never got to meet his mother, as she was turned into a myrrh tree before he was born.

All Adonis knew was being under Aphrodite's watchful eye. He spent a lot of time with her, so much so that Ares always seemed angry about it. He was a few years older than Persephone, and all the girls thought he was gorgeous. The Graces, the Muses, and most of the nymphs would try their damndest to get his attention. Adonis seemed aloof and reserved around the residents and guests of Mount Olympus. But he would intently follow Persephone with his eyes.

Persephone loved to play in the fields with her friends as a young girl. She was oblivious to the eyes that were upon her. As the youngest of Zeus' children, she knew and understood little of what was going on around her. Adonis seemed to only be more relaxed around her and always keen on getting her alone.

One afternoon, when the nymphs she used to

dance, sing, and fashion flower crowns with were called to other activities, Persephone found herself alone among the flowers. Adonis spotted her and approached her with a small smile on his lips.

"Let's play a game," he began and Persephone lit up, as she had been alone and wanting company. He led her away from the fields and into the forest. Skipping along with him and humming to herself, Persephone was enchanted by the novelty of a place she had never known. They came upon a moss-covered cave and Adonis beckoned her to come after him.

"This is a secret place Aphrodite brings me to often," he said, fidgeting with his hands and looking down at his feet. Persephone was too naive to notice the subtle shift in him. "Can I show you what we do here?"

She nodded excitedly. Adonis pressed her against one of the walls. Persephone's stomach began to hurt and she felt sick. Without warning, his lips were on hers; her stomach churned with nausea but she had no idea what was happening. He said it was a game. So she played along and kissed him back. Adonis didn't seem to mind until Persephone instantly began kissing his face and then his neck.

Suddenly, Adonis hurriedly stepped away from her, as though something struck him. Persephone was confused and feeling anxious all at the same time.

"Did I do something wrong?" Persephone asked, almost in tears, noticing Adonis getting angry. He pushed her away and ran. It was late when Persephone finally found her way home. Demeter was angry when she walked in and didn't notice or care for her daughter's tear-stained face.

I did something wrong thought Persephone. From that point forward, there seemed to be something repulsive about her. Her friends vanished and the Graces didn't like her much anymore. Her best friend Medusa also disappeared around this time, with no explanation outside of her being evil, according to Athena. She never understood.

What she did know was that no one wanted her around after that. She liked Adonis. And now because she didn't understand the game, she was left in the shadows, hoping someone would help her understand.

The Risk

There was nothing to discuss that night when
I saw you again for the first time.
What could be said?
No words of "hello" sufficed when we met.
Softer lips have never touched mine so
passionately, up against the wall; your hands
grabbing my hips to bring them closer to
yours.

No words were necessary; we consented to
this moment before. I was your dessert, a
nightcap, a sweet, easily unwrapped—
a succulent morsel melting in your mouth
With a surprise everlasting creamy center;
you must have thought I was lying boy.

Our lovemaking was a tempest, an insatiable
urge to know flesh, to know what we feel like
skin to skin
A searching; a break from the logic and
reasoning that kept us apart
I knew your body promised nothing but the
hours (and hours) of pleasure we indulged in

We shared our bodies as the sand and ocean
do
Endlessly

Wave after wave of passion overtook and
overwhelmed us

The hours you were drenched in my plentiful
waters were temporary; we could have spent
days like this.

But you couldn't stay. I couldn't stay.
I slept next to your warmth so I could bask in
your light if only once in this lifetime because
I didn't want to wait until the next one
Why the risk? Why the caution to the wind?
Why risk your heart? Your eyes begged mine
silently.

For all the times I've been too cautious, there
was a reluctance to be open to
experience...and the possibility of loving you
was far too tempting and too rich to close the
door on.

You'll always tell me it was premature;
I will keep the sound of your voice tucked in
the secret parts of my heart as something
beautiful I was allowed to have, even if it was
too soon.
As the aches in my thighs and
hypersensitivity between them subside
And I can no longer see the marks you left on
my neck,
the memory still sits in me, grateful.

Medusa, the Young Priestess

She was a beauty. Brown ringlets cascade down her back and framed her heart-shaped face. Her lips were pinkish red, as though she had eaten the most succulent pomegranate in haste. Her white robes were fresh cotton, the neckline revealing only her collarbones. A rope of twine held her together at the waist and she always kept her head covered with a white veil. When they found Medusa in the temple, the last thing they saw before she turned them to stone was blood-stained white fabric.

Persephone had been close to her from days in company with the other girls who played in the fields at the foot of Mount Olympus. There were rolling hills and fields of flowers for the ones who gathered them for crowns and potions. The forest nymphs were all too happy to have their company, the curiosity of the the young girls riddled with giggles, songs, and games. It was in such fields that Medusa and Persephone came upon each other. They had both been in search of lavender and reached for the same sprig. Immediately they both laughed and were the best of friends.

They would talk for hours about herbs and flowers, and Persephone would tell her about her loneliness as well as all the stories she had read. Medusa would tell her about the world outside Mount Olympus and her dreams of being completely dedicated to Athena. This would give Persephone the chance to talk about how much she admired Artemis. Persephone saw a little less of her as time went on because, since she was a little bit older, Medusa got her wish and became a devoted priestess of Athena as soon as she could. It made Persephone want to become a priestess too but of her beloved goddess of the hunt.

Medusa was the most faithful servant anyone had ever seen. Athena often puffed out her chest whenever anyone would comment on how clean and fresh her temples were because of Medusa, as though she was responsible.

As Medusa continued to develop into a young woman, she caught the eye of Poseidon. He was as slimy as the seaweed in the watery realm he ruled. Most anyone who was not drunk or inebriated was creeped out by him; the older goddesses were visibly cringing and uncomfortable whenever they were forced to greet him. The little girls thought he was funny but would get chastised for wanting to play with him.

Medusa kept her head down and rarely mingled with any of the male gods, as her promise to remain virginal was not one she took lightly. Poseidon didn't care though, and always tried to get near her.

Athena and Poseidon were at each other's throats at this time. They had been competing to be the patron of Athens. Athena ended up being chosen by the Athenians and this made Poseidon furious. He flooded their city as punishment. Their newly minted patron goddess merely shrugged her shoulders in response, finding his anger humorous. The god of the sea wanted to piss off Athena and was keen on doing so. He quickly realized that he could kill two birds with one stone.

One night, Medusa was alone in Athena's temple. She was sweeping up after the pilgrims of the day came to give their offerings. Humming as she cleaned, she barely noticed Poseidon moving in the shadows. The candles were suddenly snuffed out and she found herself in the dark. A chill ran up her spine seconds before she was grabbed violently by the wrist. She tried to free herself but instead, the sound of her beautiful white robes being ripped was all she could hear. Cold, slimy wet hands fondled her everywhere and she began crying. Soon, the place between her legs and entire body was in pain from being taken by Poseidon. Violently.

Athena came in the morning and was furious upon seeing Poseidon on top of Medusa, taking her for god knows what round of rape. He stood up slowly, enjoying the rage rolling off of the goddess while Medusa lay, sobbing on the floor, trying to cover herself. In a flash, Athena struck Medusa and suddenly the sound of hissing snakes filled the air.

Persephone never saw Medusa again. All she was told was that she disrespected Athena and was banished forever as a monster for her crimes. Persephone was horrified - why would Medusa do something like this?

Coming of Age Pt 1 (The Tarot)

"Not a word", he said. His voice was sharp enough to threaten.

"Do not breathe a word to anyone about today. About us. I am a very private man."

Persephone felt the giddy lightness she had coursing through her slow down, the corners of her smile faltering slightly. Hades turned to look at her behind him and met her eyes, softening his aura. As his chariot rode on, he held the reigns in one hand and caressed Persephone's cheek. She blushed so deeply it gave her brown skin a rosy tint.

"You're so special, Persephone. Everything you did tonight was beautiful. No one sees how gorgeous you are, but I do sweetie," he whispered before flashing a brilliant smile at her. Persephone looked down at her hands in her lap, embarrassed and stunned. Hades lifted her head. "Let me be your friend from a distance. Whenever you feel alone, remember who thinks highly of you. I know no one else does."

Had Persephone been older, the backhanded compliment would have registered. Hades turned fully back around to take the reigns with both hands with a smirk, leaving her to her thoughts.

As they flew undetected towards Mt. Olympus, Persephone reviewed the day she had. It was her 17th birthday and she sat at the foot of Mt. Olympus alone as usual. The only time Persephone saw anyone was for Hera's weekly (mandatory) tea time and from the shadows. She would wear her cleanest robes and brush her hair back into a tame and presentable bun. As soon as the formalities of the charade at Hera's were over, Persephone would sulk away unnoticed. No one paid her any attention and she had grown to prefer it that way. At least she thought she did. The last time anyone acknowledged her was Hades and Adonis.

Persephone shook her head as if to erase the memories that constantly replayed themselves in the back of her mind. There was a constant loop of rumination playing in her head that would make her anxious trying to find the reasons why Adonis pushed her away. It had been over a decade since she lost her innocence. She had sought solace in the library. Hours alone pouring over the scrolls and books, Persephone created her little world in her head. Stories from the mortals about princesses and queens, dragons, and knights were the places from where she constructed what life was supposed to be. For years, this worked to keep her sad little smile on her face, always trailing behind the forest nymph gathering parties, talking to herself.

Persephone was building her own story of love and longing. The Graces noticed her lips moving, her eyes looking up and her giggling to herself. And that is how everyone began to say she was going to be crazy like her mother.

She felt embarrassed when she heard those whispers and buried herself deeper into her mind. When Persephone began to blossom physically into her womanhood, her curiosity was peaked by the world of magic even more. Every birthday, she would take out her tarot card deck and hug it to her chest, thinking of Hades whom she hadn't seen since his gift. She tried to read about the deck but came up empty-handed.

Sighing, Persephone would spread the cards out on the grass at the base of a twisted knobby tree, studying them and looking at the artwork. On this 17th birthday, she was doing her spread and felt someone approach. Hurriedly, she grabbed them up.

"Why are you putting them away, sweetie?", a low voice asked. The hairs at the nape of Persephone's neck stood on end. She wanted to run but found herself tense and frozen. In the blink of an eye, Hades was standing above her, looking down at her. Persephone's stomach began to turn itself into knots. Hades knelt to be on eye level with her and placed a hand on her hair. She flinched but quickly softened into the attention. Hades noticed her body's reaction to his touch. He felt himself get turned on by her fear.

Running his calloused hand down her smooth cheek, he softly rested his hand on her chin. "Hey ma," he mused, smiling at her. Persephone gave him a shy smile in return. "I see you still have the gift I gave you so long ago. I'm so happy to see you loved them," he said. Letting go of her chin, he sat in the grass beside her and held his hand out for the deck. Persephone slowly gave her deck to him. He shuffled them expertly as she watched his every move, trying to memorize the skill.

"How much do you know about these cards?", Hades inquired looking up from the shuffling cards in his hands. Persephone muttered something. "I need you to open your mouth and speak up," he responded. She cleared her throat nervously. "I don't know a lot. I can't find much in the library." Hades smirked at her. "Let me show you a little."

He spread out the cards and explained to her the difference between the major arcana and minor arcana, the four suits, and gave her the basic meanings of the major arcana. He picked out two cards specifically as he started gathering the cards. Persephone was hanging on his every word, taking a million mental notes of his teachings.

Hades gave Persephone her deck and showed her the two cards. "This one is you, the High Priestess. She's mysterious and passive but very intuitive. Her message is that you trust your inner instincts to guide you through life. Things around you are not what they appear to be right now," he said, looking Persephone in the eyes. This was one of the few times he would be sincere with her. She blushed and looked away.

"This card is me, the Devil. He's all temptation to pleasures of the flesh. His message is all about instant gratification and the shadow side. And well, I am the god of the Underworld. It's a fitting card," Hades explained, holding back a few important details, as always. He knew better than to tell her that indulging in what feels good wasn't always wise. He gave Persephone the two cards back. "How was that lesson for you? Did that help?" She nodded her head with enthusiasm.

He stood up and brushed his clothing off. Looking down at Persephone, he held out his hand. "Don't be scared. Come with me," he said as Persephone hesitantly reached for his hand. "I want to take you somewhere for your birthday." Her eyes lit up at this. Again, he remembered her birthday.

She could feel her insides fluttering with anxiety but the attention was intoxicating. He walked her over behind the tree to his chariot. Hades climbed in and took the reigns. Persephone hesitantly put a foot in the cart. "Do you trust me?" he said, getting close enough to her face to kiss her. She nodded. He wrapped his arm around her waist and hoisted the rest of her body onto the chariot.

"Let's go celebrate your birthday, ma. No one will notice we're gone."

Temptation

Was it then a blessing to have crossed paths
with you if I find myself unable to unwind
you from the spirals in my mind?

Every impression changes in my head from
speaking so bluntly

I toe the line between formality and
decadence

Wondering if the latter negates the former, or
if such admiration encourages such arousal

If I ever wanted to accuse you of anything, I
couldn't;

I'd have to confess that rituals of flesh and
carnal desire have been made, requesting
your existence as a test of will

Remembering how well men like you
instigate sensations of life between thighs
begging to be touched

I wait to pounce, tense at the neck and just
feeling the kind of nerves felt the moment
clothing becomes optional between lovers.

Thawed By Love

A warm fire by which to melt this once icy
heart
Frozen by too many winters
We fit well; never once finding ourselves
unlatched
As a July summer morning found us laying
naked in between our lovemaking sessions
My skin, cool and flushed from speaking so
intimately with you all night, whispering at
twilight
To see the light of dawn creep across your
face
Lips parting to smile, to take mine captive

I am a puddle, softened by you
As you nudge the place in my chest I thought
I lost
You told me a story from the books your
father read to you
About boys filling themselves with sunshine
to the point of inebriation
I listened with my hands roaming every
crevice I could reach laying beside you
You feel wonderful to touch; so familiar like
someone I've been with lifetimes before

Noon rolled in, beckoning us to leave your
bed and
rejoin the world outside your door
I met your eyes to ask you how you felt
With your soft smile, you told me

You were drunk
Our hands met first as we embarked on this
new journey together
When we left what was comfortable in order
to discover the unchartered territory only
imagined
I was too shy to kiss you beneath our willow
tee, where we met when night was cascading
on the heels of sunset
But I knew to take your hand and hold on
Later, I would study you and admire how
beautiful you are; the idea of attraction
becoming a reality as I examined how your
shirt complimented your muscular chest and
shoulders
And when we retreated to your bedroom, our
nervousness invaded the space between us,
but not enough to stop caressing your face
and running my hands through your hair

Our hands met again, connecting us and
syncing us to move on in holding this
moment of purposeful sensation between our
palms
Praying the way our lips would
It was sudden, our adventure into intimacy
Bodies intertwined, tongues exploring each
other's mouth
Breathing each other in deeply
Having you inside me, feeling myself
wrapped around you
Has left this wordsmith at a loss for a method
in which to fashion expressions

A poet speechless for all I could ever say can
only be heard in our intimate moments
Naked...bare
Innocent...pure
I just want to look at you all day, and lose
myself in the abyss of your pupils
Float forever in the ocean of your irises
Pretend I am searching for a seam in your
skin and delicately travel the bodyscape
encasing your divinity
Making love to you is incredible.

Coming of Age Pt. 2
(Persephone Disrobed)

Persephone had never been this far from Mt. Olympus before. She quietly wrung her hands in her robes, worried about being out without permission. _What would my mother do if she found out?_

She played countless scenes of how it would turn out for her if Demeter caught wind of this adventure. Hades could feel her anxiety rising behind him. He took the reigns with one hand and placed his hand on her head. Without looking at her, he spoke.

"Relax, Persephone. I can feel your fear from here. Forget about everyone in Mt. Olympus and just have fun today. Can you do that for me, ma?"

Persephone took a deep breath. She did her best to settle her nerves. Looking out of the chariot, she focused on watching the human world come into view. It took her breath away to see their world flying by her, and soon she was immersed in seeing the rivers, oceans, and landmasses as they kept flying. Hades cleared his throat as the chariot began slowing down.

"We're getting close to our destination. The one thing I forgot to tell you is that we have to undergo a bit of a transformation to go hang out with my friends. We're going to temporarily become humans," he said to her.

Persephone's eyes widened in fear and excitement. She had always wondered what it would be like to be a human but now being presented with the prospect was overwhelming.

The chariot came to a complete stop, softly landing in a clearing in the forest of the unfamiliar land Hades brought them to. "Will it hurt?" she asked. Hades chuckled. "Not at all. What I need you to do for me is imagine the most beautiful woman you can in your mind. Close your eyes."

Persephone let her eyelids flutter closed. Hades took her hand and guided her out of the chariot. She focused on the image in her mind - images of The Graces and several nymphs floated through her mind until Aphrodite came into view. A small smile danced on her lips. *This is my chance to be as beautiful as her*, she thought.

Hades changed in an instant to a more youthful version of himself. Then his eyes settled on Persephone. He was curious to see what she would become. "Take a deep breath," Hades whispered. He snapped his fingers and she transformed into a wheat-colored version of a young Aphrodite. Her hair was auburn instead of blonde and it cascaded down her back. Eyes still closed, Persephone wrung her hands slightly and spoke.

"Am I changed?"

Hades took in the sight of her, noticing how her new curvy body seemed to protest against the inadequate size of her old robes. His cock twitched at the thought of touching her body. *Not yet*, he advised himself. Hades cleared his throat.

"Open your eyes."

Persephone's eyes snapped open and she looked down at her body. She was in awe of the womanly curves and hue of her skin, the reddish brown tint to her flowing locks, and her dainty hands. "How do I look?"

"Simply gorgeous. Now let's get you something pretty to wear and go have fun."

Now being on earth, they had to travel on foot to their destination. After getting Persephone beautiful red silk robes to wear, Hades took her to his favorite tavern in Delphi, Philia & Eros. There they would meet his friends, often an assortment of gods and demigods who had come down to have some fun with the humans and enjoy something other than divinity.

The tavern was dimly lit by lanterns and a couple of candles throughout the establishment. Persephone unconsciously slipped her hand into Hades. He was slightly shocked by this but squeezed it lightly to provide the reassurance she sought. He scanned the place and spotted a group of his regulars, then walked towards them with Persephone following.

"Look at what we have here!" A rosy-cheeked man with a mess of dirty blonde curls greeted the two additions to the group.

"Hades, how fun of you to join us tonight! And who's this delicious morsel you've got with you?", the man said, licking his lips. Hades narrowed his eyes at him before resuming his composure.

"Oh shut up, Apollo!" he responded in a jovial tone. "Must you be so loud and belligerent all the time?"

"Only when I'm two pitchers of sangria in and Daphne is nowhere in sight!"

Hades shook his head amused before greeting the rest of the men and their harlots. "This is Rosalie, my guest for the night. It is her birthday and I wanted to show her a good time," he said, introducing Persephone to the group. She was surprised that he gave her a fake name, but simultaneously relieved to be hiding behind another personality. Maybe for a night, she could be anyone but herself.

After introducing themselves to the group, the night went on. The musicians arrived at the tavern and kicked the volume and energy up several notches. Persephone was still shy, sitting next to Hades and wanting to disappear from the anxiety she felt. He turned to her and gave her a mug.

"Have some of this, my dear," Hades told her. Persephone was hesitant but curious. "Go on, princess. I promise it'll help you have fun." With that, she brought the mug to her lips and tasted the liquid. It was sweet and warm to her tongue, with a hint of spice. Her chest began to feel warm and fuzzy. "Good, right? It's the finest pomegranate sangria you'll ever have."

Steadily, Persephone drank the contents of the mug and set it down. Soon after, one of the women who hung out with their group came over to her. The music had begun to play at a lively tempo. Persephone took a step and wobbled a bit. "Easy there, girl," the woman said to her. The woman took the mug out of her hand and put it on the table. Persephone felt insecure about moving her body so at first she stood to the side and watched the women dance in a flurry of skirts and movement. She closed her eyes and felt the percussion vibrate through her body, making it impossible not to sway.

"C'mon girl. You can't stand there all night", the woman who had taken her mug said.

Persephone opened her eyes. "I can't dance." The woman smirked. "Take my hand and close your eyes. Let your body move."

She took a deep breath and closed her eyes again. All Persephone felt were the drums reverberating off her body as she moved to the music. She felt every muscle in her body loosen and move fluidly. Soon, Persephone was improvising, staying in tune with the music. She opened her eyes and the women were in front of her dancing. Something inside Persephone took over and she began to dance around them, imitating them. The others took notice and began clapping for Persephone to keep going.

Hades' eyes followed her body as he licked his lips and adjusted himself as he grew aroused following the movements of her body. One of the drummers began to clap for Persephone. One of the dancers looked at her and it was like a challenge was being proposed by her eyes.

Persephone accepted and they began to dance with each other, with attitude, with passion. The band was excited, especially the singers, who had begun to cheer them on. By this point, Persephone had relinquished control of her body and let it go with the emotion. When the music stopped, Persephone sat down on the floor where she stood as the crowd erupted in cheers and claps. Hades came to her and picked her up, hugging her in his arms.

He nuzzled his face in her neck, and Persephone's body quickly became covered with goosebumps.

"You are gorgeous. That was beautiful," he whispered before guiding her back to the bar. Persephone felt so alive at that moment and beamed at him.

"Really?!"

"Yes. You are so sexy when you dance like that." Hades gave her another drink as the band began filling the air with syncopated beats and haunting vocals. The crowd came back alive as well as the dancers. Hades held onto Persephone and pressed her against his body. She swayed her hips as each drum beat was struck by the percussionists. After a while, Hades led her away from the crowd to a room in the back of the bar. It was dimly lit and had a platform with a chaise lounge on it.

"Persephone. Can I show you how beautiful you are?" Hades whispered to her. Persephone was on his arm, feeling a little lightheaded from the alcohol coursing through her body. She looked up at him and nodded furiously.

He walked her up to the platform and sat her on the chaise. Hades pulled a gold silk robe from underneath it. "Take your clothes off and put this on," he said to Persephone. She violently blushed at this. "But then I'll be naked," she responded sheepishly. "How else would you be as beautiful as those marble sculptures and drawings throughout the city? I remember you staring at them on our way in."

Persephone fidgeted with the robe in her hands nervously. She wrestled internally with wanting to be like one of those naked women but felt ashamed of being naked in front of her uncle.

"What if someone finds out?"

Hades smirked. "It'll be our little secret. Here," he gestured, pulling a pitcher and mug from under the seat she was on and pouring a drink, "This will help you relax. I'll step out to get some pencils so that you can undress alone."

He handed her the mug, stroked her hair, stepped down from the platform, and went looking for a sketchbook and pencils. Persephone stared at the cup in her hands and hesitantly took a sip. She had a good amount of the sangria before that buzzing feeling coursed through her again. Persephone put down the mug and with it, her inhibitions. As she stood, she let her clothing drop to the floor. Her heart was racing as she quickly put the robe on and sat on the chaise.

Hades came back in moments later. He smiled at her, pleased that she had obeyed his request. "I'm going to sit in front of you and sharpen my pencils. You are going to take off your robe and recline naturally on the lounge."

Persephone's fingers nervously went to the openings of her robes. She took a deep breath and let the robe slip off. Hades looked up at her and his jaw slightly dropped. She smiled, proud for once as he studied each curve from head to toe.

"Your mouth is open, Hades," she said with a slight giggle. He finally closed his mouth.

"You are quite the inspiring view. Your body is amazing."

She blushed. "Thanks."

During the session, they barely spoke, as though a syllable uttered would make the tension precipitate. Persephone felt Hades' eyes study every inch of her skin, scanning, analyzing, calculating with his eyes squinted and pencil held out to measure her. Their eyes met and Hades lowered his hands, letting his eyes sweep over her

"You are quite exquisite Persephone. I don't mean to make you uncomfortable but I am very impressed by the details of your body. To be honest, I'm breaking into a sweat drawing you."

Persephone felt herself grow hot all over her body, the heat prickling at her skin and making her blood rush. She was taken off guard by these sensations, as she had never felt this way. Persephone shifted in her seat and was shocked by how wet she was getting between her legs.

"I'm not quite sure how to respond, Hades."

"I'm so sorry Persephone. Please forgive my forwardness. It was not my intention to offend you," Hades said, feigning sheepishness but internally thrilled at her reaction.

"Let's finish up here. I want to show you this drawing."

The air was so thick that Persephone felt it hard to breathe with his eyes on her. After some time, Hades put down his pencil and looked up at Persephone. She was falling asleep on the chaise. He wanted to climb on top of her so badly but knew that she'd already be sober and completely freaked out. *Patience*, he muttered to himself, *you'll have her soon*. Hades got up and touched her face softly. She jolted awake and suddenly was embarrassed by her nakedness. Persephone sat up straight and quickly covered herself with the robe. He smirked.

"You're gorgeous. This will always be our secret," he said to her with a hand on her shoulder. "Can I touch you?" Hades said as Persephone sat still. She was in the robe and it had slipped off the other shoulder. Her instinct was to say no but she felt powerless in Hades' presence.

"Yes."

He stood Persephone by the waist and when Hades turned her to face him, he untied her robe. Sliding his hands inside, he took the robe off slowly, as though he was unpeeling it from her skin. Holding Persephone's naked body, he traced her clavicles down her neck and along her stomach. Hades' finger trailed down her abdomen and lingered at the bottom of it.

"I could make you even curvier if I put a baby in here. Would you like that?" Hades whispered to her.

Involuntarily, Persephone couldn't help biting her bottom lip, her body breaking out into goose bumps as his finger caressed her skin. Without warning, he pulled her closer and kissed her neck, his fingers sliding down towards her pussy and his other hand pressing her naked body to his. Persephone's body went rigid as a plank of wood. Hades knew he had gone too far. He gingerly put her robe back on as she stood there frozen, processing what just happened. *I'm a whore*, she thought. She wasn't sure why she reacted that way but it must mean she's a whore. At least that's what her mother would say if she knew.

As if nothing happened, Hades stepped off the platform without a word and offered Persephone his hand.

"Come, let me show you the picture."

Persephone felt nervous and deeply ashamed. *Maybe I shouldn't have had so much of that drink,* she thought. She took his hand and stepped off the platform and was led to where Hades had been seated. He picked up the sketchbook. Turning to the page, he says, "You'll never believe that this is who you are."

She let out a gasp as he showed her a beautiful sketch of herself on the chaise. Persephone blushed deeply at this. "You're my beautiful little secret," Hades mused as she looked at herself. She felt pride and a pang of pain, knowing that he had drawn her in the body that she wanted, not the one she was always in.

Persephone felt herself pulled back to her reality as Hades landed the chariot at the base of Mt. Olympus. He helped her out. As soon as her feet touched the ground, she transformed back into her original mahogany skin. Persephone cringed internally.

Before he got back into his chariot, Hades grabbed Persephone by the shoulders. She felt scared but swallowed her trepidation.

"Never tell anyone about our trip. They will never believe you," Hades said in an almost menacing tone. The hairs on the back of her neck stood up. Without another word, he mounted the chariot and took off. Persephone was left there alone.

What am I going to tell my mom? she panicked, realizing how late it was. Persephone had no idea what time or day it was after the experience with Hades. As she walked back to the palace, she heard people running towards her. *I've been caught*, she thought in a frenzy. The men that were running rushed past her. Suddenly she heard someone, a woman, screaming at the top of her lungs. Persephone began to run with the men, eventually stopping one of them outside of the gates.

"What happened?" she asked out of breath.

"Aphrodite is losing her mind. We need to go help her."

"Why?" Persephone asked, startled.

"Adonis has been killed."

The man kept running as Persephone sank to her knees, her heart shattering as Aphrodite's screams filled the air. Just like that, her adventure with Hades was overshadowed by tragedy. She began to sob, mourning the death of the person she thought loved her.

Esa Mujer Esta Bomba

Her hands are the first thing they notice as
she adjusts the hem of her white skirt
They study her physique, her top clinging to
her every curve
Every moment is measured, precise and
artful
As though her very being were paint and this
world, her canvas
Dark brown eyes gaze at the drums from
beneath a wild mess of hair
That shakes when she moves her head along
with the rest of her body

She was born to dance
Born to open channels of movement at every
jam she goes to
At her full height, she is full of presence
A flame dancing on a wick that cannot
contain her
When the guitarist strums his cuatro
The percussionists start beating barriles

She is on fire
Her body moves to each beat, each rhythm
Skillfully weaving in and out of each
syncopated pulse in the ground
She has erupted
Open and fluid; becoming bigger than herself
In communion with the sounds
As the bangles on her wrists speak with her
clapping to the music

She is the only one dancing in the middle of
the room
The clave speaks to her, and tells her it's time
She propositions the drummer, her skirt
bunched up in her hands
She looks at the primo, challenging their skill
Her hips begin to move slowly, teasing,
whispering
Can you keep up?
All at once, she becomes a fury
Her footsteps become a map of where she's
been as the dust lifts around her
The drummer goes wild in an attempt to
contest with the dancer
The crowd is clapping, shouting, and
cheering her on
Habla! Habla! Habla!
The tempo quickens
She is unquenchable
The drummer smiles at her as she stops and
stares
Bowing down to them for being a worthy
companion

Tu Cuerpo (August 2008)

I studied the details of his sleeping body,
watching the gentle rise and fall of his chest.
The morning was still a glowing twilight,
slowly rubbing the dark blush of night lighter
by the moment. The silence of a sleeping city
was profound, save for the night owls, night
shift people, and similar situations like the
one in my bed. The sheets hugged the curves
of my naked body as I propped my head up
with my left hand.

He slightly stirred and his eyes fluttered
open. He caught me looking at him and gave
me a sleepy smile. I moved closer to him and
began to trace the side of his torso, brushing
my fingers slowly over every crevice.

"I could write about your body for days, pa,"
I said making my way to his hips. He smiled
at me.

"Please do."

I followed the contours along the side of his
torso, and continued upward, reaching his
clavicles.

"Your body is an ancient text of haikus,
carelessly left unrevised," I whispered before
getting on top of him, straddling him, and

hovering over him. His eyes looked up at me, gazing at me, studying my body from the angle he was at. I lowered myself so that my face was near his.

"Where are they written, ma?" he asked gently, reaching out and holding my hips. He caressed the small of my back with one hand, holding me steady with the other.

"I count the syllables buried in your clavicles, the ones submerged in your candy perfume skin…" I said, kissing him slowly starting at his heart and trailing down his abdomen. He let go of my hips so I could slide down his body. I teased the piece of skin right above his waistline. He tensed up, trying to relax but I could feel his breath become excited. I looked up at him, mischievously. I came back up to meet his lips and searched his mouth for his soul, moving around his tongue, rummaging to find a way to hold on to the passion surging through our bodies.

I could feel the heat rising in his body, the tension in him holding himself steady to prevent from exploding. This is how we did it best, excruciatingly slow; taking great care to touch every single taunt muscle, every limb aching to be intertwined with its match. He had a lot of control though. His hands were paintbrushes, gliding along the canvas of my inner thighs, making my heart race as I continued to kiss him slowly. His palette of colors changed from the mocha of my skin to the pinks and reds of my insides. My eyes rolled back as I just rode the waves of pleasure reaching my toes and the ends of every hair on my body.

I felt all of him and he maintained his pace in and out of me. I felt myself release every time he plunged into me; I was so aware of his sweat, the musk of his manhood infiltrating my lungs and consuming me. I closed my eyes as he pressed his heart against mine, still moving rhythmically in and out of me.

I got increasingly more and more excited as he picked up his pace. My body tensed up as every stroke brought me closer. My mind went blank, reminding me of the peace I'd find in that void at the end of yoga class.

A voice inside me commanded me softly, "Let go." I breathed in, the pleasure washing over me like sunshine. I almost leaped out of my skin. Every boundary that separated my soul from his disappeared. We climaxed together, intertwined and involved in this intensity. Nothing else existed outside of this moment; both of us pouring into each other, with no restrictions. He was focused on me. My eyes were still shut, after he had gone soft and was on top of me. I could feel his eyes boring into me. He placed his hand on my face.

"Look at me."

My eyes fluttered open. His brown eyes stared at me. it was one of the first times I remember truly looking at anyone in the eyes. I felt myself get choked up, but swallowed hard, letting myself only blink away the tears.

"Why do you avoid looking at me?" he whispered, never breaking our stare.

"When someone looks you in the eyes, they can see into you," I responded after a short pause. His eyes widened slightly.

"It amazes me that a nude model could be so guarded and hidden. It's like the less you have on, the more you cover up," he said thoughtfully.

Telegram to Adam

Hello Lover. (stop)
This is how I pray. (stop)
Facing east; sunset drenched back meditating
on rising moons as you enjoy being in the
middle of me. (stop)
Painting beds with our watercolors, and still
hanging them out to dry. (stop)
Dancing naked in your bed and doing all of
your favorite things. (don't stop)
The one transgression we cannot resist; you
whisper litanies in my ear. (don't stop)
Blasphemous mouth of mine as I pronounce
you the divine; the one bringing me close to
death while my body vibrates with purpose.
(don't stop)

The original sin, so to speak. (stop
The angels filed complaints that their music
could not drown out throaty moans sounding
more heavenly (don't stop))
The ultimate temptation; the fruit offered by
your Eve. (stop)
Papaya. (stop)

The unmatched experience of knowing God.
(stop)
We both want a taste. (don't stop)

This Body, This Metaphor

Poetry
Not just a way to show mastery of verbally
manipulative Jedi mind tricks
But my way of expressing the metaphors that
breathe around me
A blade of grass is human
Similes raining on me like a weeping sky

Sometimes sensual sensations on skin sedate
or stir the titillating tremors of tempting
territories not known previously
I contemplate my awareness of solitude as I
spend hours in my own confines of creature
comforts
Learning to co-exist with the watcher within,
who beckons me to perch myself on the other
end and gaze into her eyes

I knock back memories without a chaser,
recognizing that I must ingest that fungus
among us even if I am momentarily ill
Clawing at this flesh is a wild thing of sorts
Seeking to travel multidimensionally to every
place I've ever loved:
- That little warm bar on a corner in Spanish
  Harlem
- The middle of a dusty sculpting studio
  floor, a wooden box draped with fabric as I
  inspire creations of earthen mediums
- Black-top cracking rooftop in Sunset Park

- A stone step on the stairs of Union Square
  as the allure of the horizon pulls the sun
  closer

In the space between me, you, us
I dance within the sacred and the profane
Where poetry becomes intercourse becomes
poetry imitating life

There isn't so much as a drop of regret nor
resignation to the influences of learning how
to traverse the basins of your clavicles
Wandering carefully along the landscape of
your torso, discovering valleys in your
abdomen
As I rest my lips in the canyon of your hip
bone
(I will kiss you there softly; to tell you that
you are divine)
I trust that the apex of the arch my body
creates over the threshold of this place we
cross over from duality to simplicity is held
stable by your hand

Sometimes we don't even touch
Breathing this way.

Zeus & Hades

The crazy bitches fuck the best.

Persephone laughed and laughed, giggled, and hiccuped. This little girl was already tipsy, Hades thought.

Zeus came over at the request of Demeter. "Go check on our daughter. Hades is here."

He smirked at Persephone as he went around the bar and stood in front of the man who would eventually take her for himself.

"We call it a transfer of property. She belonged to me before she ever belonged to her mother. She is mine to give as I please."

His eyes grew wide as he drank in the words of his brother.

Zeus continued. "She's crazy like her mother, so they will only believe what we say happened tonight and thereafter."

His niece was looking delicious tonight, a young pretty little thing. Doe-eyed and strikingly gorgeous. Hades could stare at her all night, his eyes hungrily lapping up the places his tongue would soon be. He remembered the stolen moments they had spent in Delphi and the restraint he had then.

Tonight, he would claim what he wanted most. Soon. When she's too drunk to know what happened to her.

"Another pitcher of sangría, please."

"That's the devil's juice, take it easy there!" Poseidon roared from the other end of the bar, his cold slimy hands nearly undressing the nymph hanging off him.
Hades narrowed his eyes at him, then darted them to his left, seeing if Persephone had heard him. She was giggling even more, her cheeks up high by her eyes. Her cheekbones were perfectly contoured, sculpted like the rest of her. A goddess who was about to be his pillow princess.

Mine. The words kept reverberating in his head as he shifted his eyes in front of him. She hadn't touched the drink her father so generously poured for her. Hades gently put his hand on her back and pushed the drink closer to her.

She immediately shook her head. "I think I've had enough," Persephone whispered to him.

"It gets more fun the more you drink. Remember how much fun you had at Philia & Eros with me? Keep drinking, you'll have even more fun," he said, using a little more force than he meant to. It was enough to make her stiffen slightly under his hand. She relaxed quickly and started sipping her drink.

"Good girl."

Zeus brought Hades a bottle of Negra Modelo with a wink and a smirk.

"She's a little one. Take it easy on her."

Hades tipped his black fedora to his wingman. This was too easy. He sipped slowly too, because it wasn't him who had to be drunk for this. His pretty little prey soon would be lubricated sufficiently to slip inside her without protest. Later, when they all found out what happened, it would be her fault for not knowing how to hold her liquor.

Invitation

I was wild in your midst
I was so deeply taken by you like teeth
sunken into a succulent fruit, letting the juice
run down my chin as I savored you

I can still feel your eyes on me as my body
slithers
I saw the way you stare at me, watching me
dance
I can only but slightly catch a glimpse of your
eyes from beneath the brim of your hat,
puffing on your cigar, piercing me with that
look of yours
I wanted you the minute I saw you;
fantasized about fucking you as you did the
same on your end

I moved to your voice as though you were
beckoning
My hips come hither to plate-tectonic-slide
past yours between my sheets
What choice do you make when the offer is
staring at you, studying the way the clothing
hangs off your curves, imagining you without
them?
You are a decadent dream of gluttonous
delight; I have no shame in indulging
Who could resist you?

Take me as yours; fuck me hard when I'm
asking you to go faster

Grind slowly in and out of me, whispering in
my ear, asking me to tell you how good all of
you feels
Baby, let me blindfold you, tease you a little
Lick your shaft up and down until you're
begging to be let go
Let me straddle you and ride you, rocking my
hips to your rhythm moving into me
I want to make your eyes roll back, pa
Flexing my muscles around your cock,
making myself feel that much tighter
Feels good, doesn't it?

Make my pussy quiver, shake, tremble,
convulse, throb for you
Unleash my rivers, my waterfalls flowing as I
release in ecstasy
Make sure you're doing laundry in the
morning 'cause I'm soaking right through
your sheets
How's that for wet, pa?
I'll put you out of commission, wear you out
until you're ready for round two

The Conquest

Hades needed her to be somewhat coherent for the journey he had planned for them.

Everyone at the party was drunk beyond belief. Leave it to Dionysus and his lunatics to throw the booziest debauchery he'd been to in some time. Hades roamed the earth plenty but had stayed on the fringes of the Olympians' world and pleasantries. He thought most of the gods were a waste of time and space - immature godchildren with serious Daddy issues. Persephone was the only one he needed to satisfy his insatiable appetite for innocence and that which had not yet been corrupted.

The music competed with the roar of the crowd, so he had to get closer to her. His hot breath on her neck immediately made her eyes roll back as if about to be possessed.

"Why don't we get out of here and find somewhere quieter?" he said to her, moving the pitcher and glass away from her. Persephone's eyelids seemed heavy for her but she found the strength to snap them open. "I could use some air."

Hades stood up first. He then took her hand and arm gently to help her out of her seat. Partly because he didn't know exactly how drunk she was and partly to minimize any attention on them should she fall or stumble because she was drunk. She gripped his hand tightly, holding on steady as the room spun and she swayed on her feet. In his last act of mercy, he stopped on the way out at a bathroom. After emptying her bladder, she was a little more alert but still under the influence.

The cool air hit their skin as they stepped out into the night. Darkness had fallen and the only lights came from the party, the stars, and the moon. Hades took a deep breath and scanned the field before him. A white narcissus seemed to glow from the base of a twisted knobby tree. Persephone clung to his arm for support as she giggled to no one in particular. She was chatting and talking incessantly to Hades about shit he cared little about. *She talks way too fucking much,* he thought as he walked toward the flower.

"Oh! What a pretty flower!" she exclaimed in a whisper. She had no idea why she was whispering but Hades made her feel like a little girl who didn't know better. Admittedly, Persephone was barely a maiden and everything she knew was overshadowed by her time in Mount Olympus and by her uncle. She was supposed to be scared of him - and she was. But the rising panic in the pit of her stomach was familiar enough to not register its warning to her. Hades made her feel this way her whole life. According to Aphrodite, that's what love felt like.

They got closer to the narcissus. Finally able to undo the restraints he'd put on himself for years, Hades let Persephone's hand slide into his. He brought her hand to his lips and began to kiss it slowly, making his way to her wrist. His other hand grabbed her other wrist firmly but gently. Persephone's body began to react and she could not help but pant. She'd never been with a man before, not in this way. She wanted to protest - this felt wrong but she vaguely remembered how she reacted after Hades sketched her to his touch. As Hades slowly pushed her up against the tree and pressed his body to hers, the delicious flames dancing and warming her core began spreading through her wet folds. She forgot the shame she had and began to lose herself in the ecstasy of the moment.

Hades put his head in the crook of her neck and breathed her in deeply. His cock twitched and pressed against the restraint of his pants. He could smell the scent of jasmine and her arousal, intoxicating him. Slowly leaving a trail of hot wet kisses on her neck, he pinned her hands above her head and headed down. Her beautiful breasts begging to be freed, Hades skillfully pulled them out with his mouth and promptly took her nipples in her mouth. Persephone purred with pleasure at this. He was going to lose control if she kept reacting this way to his touch.

He found her pussy and without warning, slid a finger inside her. She gasped, in shock and in heat, unsure of what he was going to do but knowing it felt divine. *What else would this feel like with a god?*

Goddess, she's so fucking wet. Hades felt a wave of pride at how his conquest was melting in his hands. *I want to taste her*, he thought to himself moments before picking up the pace of his finger, dropping down to his knees, and taking her with his mouth. Persephone moaned, and it drove him crazy. He kept sucking her pussy and pumping his finger furiously in and out. She was so close to climaxing.

Persephone felt a warm euphoric sensation start to build deep within her. His one finger was not enough to reach the wanting and need inside her. The woman in her woke up and was demanding a release. Hades stopped suddenly. Persephone opened her eyes. He was staring at her intently for a few moments. She almost admonished him for stopping until he stood up, took her hand and put it on his hard cock. Hades felt the trepidation in her as she felt his erection.

He cared little about this, desiring only to have her pretty little mouth on it. Persephone felt herself falling until she was suddenly on her knees looking up at Hades. She was silently equal parts aroused and scared; she'd never been in this position before and had not ever seen a man this close. He took her by the chin and moved her closer to his cock before pushing it into her mouth. Persephone obliged and let Hades control this. He was in control at all times.

He pumped in and out of that pretty little mouth of hers, all hot and wet like her pussy. Pulling out, he was ready to feel her now. He pulled her up by her chin and pressed her against the tree again. Her breath hitched in her chest as he placed one hand on her throat and the other on her hip.

"I've never done this before," she whispered as if confessing something shameful. He smirked.

"All the more reason that you learn what this is from me," he whispered back before moving his hand back to her pussy. Working her back up to a sloppy wet mess, he positioned himself at her entrance. Without warning, he plunged into her with a grunt.

Persephone's eyes flew open. She felt the pain of his big cock having rammed into her. He steadied himself and grabbed her hips in his hands. Though she wanted to beg him to take it slow, the words hardly made it out of her mouth. Hades fucked her hard. He slid in and out of her, enjoying the feeling of her pussy. Or rather, his pussy.

"You like that shit, huh?" He rasped out at her as she squirmed under him. Persephone had stopped feeling pain and her body had taken over. Hades slapped against her bottom as he took her hard and fast. All she could feel was a rising heat growing ever quickly and steadily as he was relentlessly fucking her. Her pussy was dripping copious amounts of wetness and she swore as he carried on. The pleasure he was giving her was too much. Persephone began to feel herself climax. Her breathing became more ragged as she savored how his cock was stuffed in so deeply, filling her pussy up. *It felt so good, my fucking God.*

The orgasm hit deep and long. Persephone rode her climax and his cock, never wanting the sensation to stop. He found another spot inside her and stroked her into multiple orgasms. Hades wanted her pussy to milk the shit outta his dick; her contracting slick walls were incredible.

He could barely contain his own release - years of watching over this pretty young

Black thing and playing the long, excruciatingly slow long game were finally culminating in this tight ass pussy who belongs to no one but him. "I want to fill you up, you're so fucking hot and tight," he said, talking her through her next orgasm. Her pleasure was so much for him that he had to oblige. Hitting her deepest spot, Hades unloaded his seed and let go of all that anticipation and hard work he'd put in.

Promptly he slipped out of her, suddenly self-aware. He'd let himself slip fucking her up against the tree and not waiting to take her home. Persephone whimpered at the sudden loss of his cock. She was not as self-aware and her knees buckled under her weight. Hades caught her just in time after pulling up his pants. He quickly scanned around them with his eyes. The party raged on and no one heard them. Chuckling to himself, he threw Persephone over his shoulder and ripped the narcissus out of the earth. There, a small hole grew and opened the ground up in a fury, the molten red insides of the earth staring back at him.

"Let's go home, ma."

Eros

"Eros in Greek mythology was the primordial god of sexual love and beauty. Eros is passionate love, with sensual desire and longing. Plato refined his definition: Although eros is initially felt for a person, with contemplation it becomes an appreciation of the beauty within that person or even becomes an appreciation of beauty itself. Eros refers to the romantic love that has tremendous passion, physical longing, deep intensity, and intimacy."

How do I love you?
Through the pores of your skin,
the feeling of having you deep within…
that's how I love you.

My hips sync with yours, moving in and out of each other as our passion collapses all boundaries of time, order, and limitations.

Asi te amo.

That sexual wanting; the longing to touch your body, to caress each part of your torso as my fingers graze every inch of you. My hands aching to traverse your hip bones, to have my lips on your bare naked flesh as I kiss my favorite parts along the way. Aroused by just the thought of your eyes piercing me, that deliberate stare that follows the curves of my body, your bedroom eyes seducing me even as I stand fully clothed, still. Still waiting to be unwrapped by your nimble fingers as they unlatch, unhook, unfasten, unbutton, and unravel the fabrics that keep your skin from mine.

You are burning slow on the end of a blunt on a Friday night; creeping like a chill up my spine, smoldering right before I clip you and enjoy every influence of your high.
Maybe you heard it through my body. As our bodies intertwined and interlocked, was there not a conversation made between two on the edge of leaping out of their skin?

What of the passion I took you with?

I love your clavicle, elegant neck, and mounds of torso deep. Wanting you inside me, deep. That kind of love. And after your body ceases motion, after your breathing has become even and steady, you lay beside me in peace. I am drawn to smile softly at you and gently caress you. There is repose and resignation to sweet surrender in this bed we've made ours. We pause in the twilight of dawn in between sheets; we are weary wanderers of the wind, often never in the same place where the sun rose on us.

We could spend days like this but could never stay. It was a fortunate collision of realities we instigate sometimes when the

moon is full, bodies in union for just that
moment.

First and foremost:
Fuck you.

Degraciao.

What I Remember

The earth swallowed me. Someone was screaming incessantly but I could barely make out who. It was far away yet in my head. I was far away from myself. All appeared as though I was staring at the world around me through a veil of water. Rubbing at my eyes furiously, a rising panic overwhelmed me. I swallowed hard to fight the feeling.

Everything came back into focus. I was by the willow tree again, staring at the narcissus. Cocking my head to the side, the flower seemed strange. I bent down to look more closely and I noticed it was wilting on the stem. That wasn't normal. A chill ran down my spine. Immediately I stood up and sprinted in the direction of the palace.

I remember the sangria creeping up on me as I sat at the bar next to Hades. It wasn't the first time I felt the giggles I couldn't control. I felt so grown up sitting at the bar. The music was lively and there was furious dancing as the drugs and the spirits worked on the party.

Aphrodite was dancing with Dionysus, pressing her body up against his, as more wood was added to the nearby fire pit. The crackling of the wood made Aphrodite's head snap back, her eyes seemed to dart around until she found what she was looking for. Ares was in the arms of two maenads, his hands shamelessly roaming their bodies as they laughed and sang. He still had his wits about him, and when he locked eyes with Aphrodite, I swear I saw fire in his eyes. As though her skin was suddenly burning from her dance with Dionysus, she recoiled and disappeared into the crowd.

I gazed around the room and my eyes locked briefly with Artemis. I hardly ever saw her around and suddenly felt ashamed that I wasn't pure enough to be her priestess. She seemed worried as she looked at me and then to Hades. I thought she was going to come over for a moment, but when I looked again, Artemis was gone.

My eyes blurred a little as I was brought back to where I sat by Hades, with his hand on my lower back. The warmth of his palm and the pressure of his fingers felt almost electric on my skin. No one ever touched me like Hades. He was so firm it was nearly painful. In Delphi, his touch was much more delicate.

The power behind his grip was restrained. I felt my pulse quicken as his hand kept traveling to my hips and ass. My breath hitched in my chest when he cupped a handful of my asscheek with his hand. I felt both excited and scared. This was bold for me. I wanted to frantically push him away and scan the room for anyone who could see us like this. My body began to cringe as I felt his hand grope me. The sangria blunted the panic as my blood felt warmer. If my mother saw me, she would call me a whore.

The tension between us was forbidden. The God of the Underworld was by far the most dangerous confidant I could have. I ached for more.

Gazing out into the crowd, I watched bodies gyrate with want and desire, sweating and rubbing each other madly. My pussy throbbed at the idea of rubbing my body hard against Hades. I snapped out of it. *What was wrong with me?*

I shook my head to refuse another drink, wanting to keep the last bit of myself conscious. He dug his fingers into my skin so hard that I thought I'd have bruises.

"Have another one," he ordered.

I felt my body stiffen as if in protest before reluctantly taking another sip. My thoughts sloshed together.

I can't remember how we got outside. I looked back at the party and saw the color slowly draining from the walls, and the fruit rotting on the tables.

I wanted to scream and found that I couldn't. I tried to run but I could not move my body. My breathing became uneven and quick as I tried to remember why I was out here and where Hades was. Suddenly compelled, I ran to the narcissus before stopping short of the tree beside it.

There, I saw myself pressed up against the trunk and Hades was pressed up against mine. I watched him take me and heard our sounds of pleasure. I felt my body react to this. I was in disbelief mostly, shocked that Hades would take me. I was far away from myself. Had I been sober, it would have never happened.

As feverish and passionate as it was, soon Hades pulled out and buckled himself just in time to catch me from falling. Passed out, he hoisted me over his shoulder and pulled the peculiar narcissus out of the earth. The small opening this left grew with a terrific roar, an eerie silence falling on everything else. Hades' chariot appeared with four magnificent black horses at the ready.

He placed my body in the cart and took off with me. Deeper and deeper into the earth, he journeyed as I woke up, visibly disoriented. I was far away from myself. Skilled charioteer that he was, Hades grabbed me and put me between him and the chariot while still driving. I was on the verge of freaking out as Hades reached into his pocket. I got the sudden taste of a sweet nectar-like liquid that lulled me into an intoxicated state once more. I felt through my body his cock getting hard as the cringing of my muscles relaxed under the influence.

I lost count of how many times I screamed, *oh my God, oh my God* as I rode the pleasure this forbidden love gave me. All of my spirit surrendered to him. And right then, I fell madly and hopelessly in love. I had attention. The first man to make me feel beautiful and grown. Desired. I felt important.

"Your skin looks so good next to mine," he rasped out as I giggled from the recklessness of the wild horses. The insides of the earth rushed by us as I took in the smells of it all, dirt slowly becoming sulfur and molten rock. Everything was on fire. The heat was suffocating and I found it hard to breathe. I was sober now. I was frightened and deeply ashamed of myself. Sensing my panic, Hades brought the chariot to a screeching halt. He dismounted and I got out hurriedly, backing away from him.

Hades caught me before I fell into the river behind me. Bringing me close, he attempted to drag his tongue on me again but I flinched and pushed him away. I wanted to start screaming. He was no longer smiling. His face darkened. Hades fought to maintain his grip on me but I was fierce. I heard the sound of nails ripping leather. I managed to scratch his face, drawing blood. I quickly recoiled as if surprised I did that.

I couldn't control the nervous fit of laughter that came out of me. Hades hated many things, but he especially loathed being mocked in any way. He felt a violent wave of rage rip through him and shot a glare at me, an insolent child. Before I could react, he grabbed me and yanked me hard by the arm. Within seconds, Hades ripped the last bit of my robes that had survived the trip. He pinned me to the ground from behind and immobilized me.

I tried to free my arm from his grip frantically. He took both my biceps and pulled my arms back. I struggled to free myself but Hades gripped me tighter.

"That shit was not funny!" he bellowed, shaking me violently. I was floating now, above this horrific scene, and found that the scream in my throat would not come out. Without warning, Hades dragged his tongue from the crack of my ass up my back. He pressed himself against me and stabbed himself into me, over and over. As if to punish me.

My entire body stiffened as I watched myself be raped by the love of my life.

After he emptied himself inside me, I still had some fight left in me but not enough to save myself from the grip he maintained on my arms.

"No one will ever know, or believe you. You fucking crazy slut."

I looked down at my chest and saw my chest begin to split open. The pain was unbearable but there was nothing I could do to stop it. Looking back at Hades, he had not let go of my arms as I fought. Yanking me up, he kept pulling my arms back to break me.

The sound of my flesh ripping apart was awful. My chest finally broke open and my sternum cracked from the force. All movement ceased and there was a gaping hole in my body.

Hades dragged my body to the river in front of him, the River Lethe. The river of forgetfulness.

Unceremoniously, he tossed the body into the water and walked away. I could have imagined it but I swear the lights of this godforsaken place flickered. He wiped his hands clean on his clothes, took a look to see if I was sinking, and kept walking.

Deadly Desire

I wanted to be
the Persephone to
your Hades
You lured me with the
temptation of making me a
bad girl
But failed to tell me it
required the
sacrifice of my light
Or how cold it would be
For so long
After you took my warmth.

After

Where did my caution sleep the night passion
took me for a trip in the dark valleys of
careless affections?
Did
My trembling body feel too quickly?
Heart too eager to be stolen without regard?

For my sanity
I fear
The pace of winter, mistrusting the Earth to
give me spring
When I cannot forget the loss of autumn
I am still shaking in terror
Very scared to trust the warmth of summer
will not scorch me again

I am that May night
Reluctant to reduce my love to lust like
Something dirty I wanted to make clean
Small little girl in shock
Twisted mouth, silenced scream
As my love sought to teach
This vessel so thirsty for water
Taught my tight pussy how to find pleasure
in trauma
My chest clenched in pain, exposed
Pulled back to be broken

In the wake of myself leaving this bruised
body
You were too rough for this to be kind.

Punishment enough for a disrespectful
wench, your voice almost said

It was a cold summer
Praying for the death of winter chill
To justify the fear shrouding me
In this oppressive heat
That wanted to make me proud and sexy
young thing again
How could I be reborn so prematurely
If I was still left half-dead
Half of who I was
In a bed neither of us could claim

It was spring when I died.
In what season do things like me grow again?

Survivor Speak

I speak to you from the other side
Foreign shores strange to
those who have not made it
across the River Styx
I knew enough about death
to have carried out my own
funeral rites and put a coin
in my mouth.
We love survivors because
it saves us the work of
embalming them;
half-dead is preferable.
The strength it takes to
survive is assumed to be
enough to continue in the
world of the living.

Half-Dead (She Asked For It)

My eyes snapped open. I was enveloped by an icy chill that seeped into my bones, leaving me trembling and disoriented. Lethe had become Styx and I was still in the water. Gradually, the haze of death dissipated and I was deposited on a riverbank. I looked around me and saw a dimly lit chamber engulfed in shadows. The air hung heavy with a musty scent, tinged with sulfur that stung my senses.

Groaning in pain, I pushed myself up from the cold, unforgiving ground. My chest ached and I looked down. I was horrified at the gaping wound and began sobbing, sinking to the ground again. *Did that happen? Did Hades rape me?* I thought.

After what seemed like hours, my sobs quieted and I looked around again. I quickly realized I was in the Underworld because I knew I was not alive anymore. This cavernous chamber had walls carved from ominous black rock, adorned with intricate, foreboding designs that sent a shiver down my spine.

An overwhelming sense of unease washed over me as I took in my surroundings, the realization of my solitude amplifying the despair that clawed at my chest. Figures moved in the shadows, their forms indistinct yet radiating an aura of palpable dread. Whispers, barely audible, echoed through the chamber, carrying words of despair and anguish that weighed on my soul. As I stood up and began to walk, my heart was heavy with grief and resignation. The chamber offered no solace, no escape from the suffocating darkness that threatened to consume me. Each step forward felt like a futile effort, the ground beneath me solid yet unforgiving, as if mocking my feeble attempts to find a way out.

With each passing moment, the weight of my surroundings grew heavier, pressing down on me like an insurmountable burden. The shadows seemed to taunt me, their sinister forms twisting and contorting with each flicker of movement, a reminder of the death that loomed over me.

Despair gripped me like a vice, squeezing the last remnants of hope from my weary soul. Lost in the depths of this nightmarish realm, I resigned myself to the cruel reality of my fate. Tears blur my vision as I succumbed to the overwhelming grief that engulfed me, a silent lament for the life I once knew, now lost to the unforgiving embrace of death.

A low murmur of voices snapped me momentarily out of my thoughts. I followed the sound to a dark corridor where I was shocked to see Hera, Athena, and Artemis gathered as if having a tea party. But it was nothing like the parties I had been to in Hera's chambers. It was colorless, in black, grey, white, and sepia tones. My body trembled with a mix of fear and rage as I listened to their conversation.

Hera lounged gracefully on a black velvet chaise, her gaze cold and calculating as she swirled the contents of her teacup in her hand. Athena lounged nearby with a similarly indifferent expression.

"Did you see Persephone at the party last night?" Hera's voice dripped with disdain as she recounted the scene, her lips curling into a smirk. Her voice sent a shiver down my spine.

Athena chuckled darkly, her eyes gleaming with malice. "Oh, I saw her all right. Giggling and drinking, draped all over Hades as if he were her lover."

Hera's laughter echoed through the hall, sharp and mocking. "And to think she's supposed to be the epitome of innocence and purity. What a joke."

Athena scoffed. "Persephone? Innocent? Tuh! Her best friend was Medusa and we all know what a little slut that one turned out to be. I am positively certain Persephone is a whore. Just like her mother."

My breath caught in my throat. *I thought they cared about me.* My vision blurred with tears. *Did they see how Hades was the one to have his hands all over me?*

Hera pretended to gag.

"Ugh, Demeter, la loca! What a shame to be her daughter and turn out exactly the same!"

"And did you see the way she was dressed?" Athena's voice dripped with scorn. "She practically invited trouble with that provocative robe."

I looked down at my tattered white robe that Hades had ripped. *Was it because of what I was wearing?* I thought as the shame consumed my insides.

Artemis's voice, softer and filled with genuine concern, cut through the venomous chatter. "I heard about what happened last night," she interjected, her voice trembling with emotion. "Is Persephone all right?" Hera waved a dismissive hand, her gaze cold and unfeeling. "Oh, she'll survive. But she got what was coming to her, that's for sure."

Athena nodded in agreement, her voice dripping with contempt. "She's always been so desperate for attention. It's no wonder she ended up in *that* situation."

Artemis shook her head, her expression grim. "I fear the worst. The way she was acting...it reminded me of the stories I've heard of mortals who have been...violated."
Hera chuckled darkly.

"Violated? Oh please, Artemis. That's just what they say to act like fucking victims. They all wanted it and Persephone is no different."

Wicked laughter filled the air as I was horrified by all this in the shadows. I felt uneasy and untrusting of my memories. Did I ask for it? Did Hades take what was his? Maybe it was because of Delphi? Maybe I should have never laughed at him. I wrung my hands in my robe. What happened to me?

Fall Of Persephone

When he took the sweetness from
the midsummer breeze
I felt a chill up my spine
I couldn't shake it long after it passed
My life was a sprawling garden of Eden
I laughed in morning glories
The rivers in me were babbling brooks
The warmth of the sun baked itself right into
my skin and left me golden
A meadow dressed in colors
I am still learning the names of
I was the space between the bee's knees and
pollen beds in the folds of the roses
My bosom swelled with abundance
I was fertile
I was supple

When he ripped the innocence out of my
magnolia soul
There was a gasping for air from the shock of
the force
I couldn't hear a sound
Every vibrant color became dull and gray
A shadow cast over my earth
I was froze
My mouth filled with the bitter iron taste of
blood from internal bleeding
Everything that held joy for me
began withering

My hands became clumsy and could not
fashion the flower crowns I used to make
with the forest nymphs

All of it happened slowly
Like a sickness progressively getting worse

I told Demeter that I was raped.
She hugged me and that was it.
Later she would say offhandedly
that there had been comments;
My behavior was that of
a person who had been violated.
No one thought to check if
their suspicions were confirmed.
Now that I think about it, why would they?
If they could not see themselves,
how could they see me?

My body was numb.
The sounds around me seemed lower and
barely reached my ears.
All the colors, as vibrant as they are,
were opaque and insipid.
Even the richest food
seemed nearly bland to me
Gray-colored glasses and a body slowly
became paralyzed due to my disconnect from
what was a crime scene.

My mother would look at me with a manic
smile that barely covered her grief,
her heavy cloud lingering around her.

Why, she'd asked, *aren't you smiling?*

Tú eras bien simpática.
You used to be so sweet.
Eyes glazed over, she'd ask,
"What happened to you?"
The dam behind my eyes wanted to
break and flood her; it would be in vain.
I was drowning, suffocating, shocked,
growing cold
My body was crying as my spirit slowly
wilted, fell apart, and nearly completely died.

Years of feeling my body atrophy
My hips locked stiffly into place
refusing to glide and gyrate any more
Knees that find it hard to kneel in the
meadows to gather my herbs and flowers
Taking a deep breath felt sharp;
breathing into my body was painful

My body was hurt
It ached
Is this because keeping a corpse animated
was supposed to hurt?
I was dying
I was drowning
This deep wound was hemorrhaging and
yet the drain on my soul was slow

I was lost in the darkness of my pain
Everything that had ever hurt
Was stabbing me everywhere

I stopped dancing.
I loved to dance.
I laughed less.
I loved to laugh.

A part of my soul left when he gripped me
as though to break me
I saw all of it happen from a distance
Floating above this man justifying
one of the most violent acts
Of both penetration and forced submission

Medusa's Rage

After walking for endless hours through the
caverns of this wretched place
I heard the distant sound of snakes hissing.
My hair stood on end. I wanted to turn
around but my body kept moving

I came to the place where the sound came
from and I froze
The shape of a woman with her hair
slithering in all directions had her back to me
A head full of snakes spoke and I recognized
the voice immediately

Medusa?!

"They called you a beast too, eh?
Because you tore at your skin afterward?
The way you kept screaming and wanting to
rip his eyeballs out made you ugly."

How did you know?! Did you hear me screaming?

"I bet you roared something terrible and
awesome
I bet they called you a liar when you wailed
So they stuffed your mouth with your own
bloodied clothes that he viciously ripped
from you before he raped you, right?

Calladita te ves más bonita
At least that's what they said to me

When they found me."

What happened to you?

My old friend took a drag of her cigarette
Her face pale with a sickly green tone to it
Eyes lined heavily with black charcoal
Gray tattered priestess robe that was in
shreds
She looked into a mirrorless vanity table and
Painted her lips fire
Fluffed her mane of snakes
Shielded her eyes with sunglasses and looked
at me

"I heard what happened to you, Persephone
And how did they reward you? She scoffed
The gods?
The fucking gods!?
What good will they be in delivering you
justice?
You heard the story, right?
Fuck Poseidon and Athena.
What good was it to have been her devoted
priestess when this is how I am repaid?"

"I pay the price for my violation!
I am the sacrificial lamb to petty gods!"

She spits this out, foaming at the mouth with
the rage that sits in her chest

"Who the fuck is supposed to protect us
when the goddesses step aside and let their
brothers have their way with us?
When a god rapes a mortal in the temple of
their familiar,
Who do we seek salvation from?"

"My death," Medusa ashes her smoke, "will
be inconsequential
Decorum more important than vindication

The Fates told me how this all ends
Another man finishes the job
I'll be murdered as part of his quest
Cuts my head off, and uses it as a weapon

I finally learned how to give good head."
She laughs sardonically
"How, my old friend Persephone, will they
repay you for paying the ultimate price?

I'll tell you what I became–
Vipers, diamondbacks, and Black mambas
sprung from my skull as I screamed endlessly
from the pain
The rattlesnakes shook violently as she spoke
And even if I found a brave soul to look at me
for all I became
I'd turn them to stone.
So I went to the ends of the earth and stayed
there

I am the monster
I am who should be feared
How?! Feared for how I combed my hair?
How I was dressed in my ceremonial robes?
Is it because one of the few things men fear is
rejection?
Did I humiliate a god by saying no?

A woman devoted to herself in the midst of a
god seeking revenge
Against a goddess is not the danger."

"No," she said pulling herself up to her full
height
Hair wild, hissing, ready to strike
"I am the monster because I speak the truth
I cannot be hidden so rather I am feared and
hunted

Because of your piece of shit uncle and
traitor of an aunt
Because this is how the world has been
fashioned by the head rapist in command
Why did we ever think anyone would be
safe?"

The Shit The Patriarchy Is On

The shit that made the patriarchy rise and
violate the rest of us was and is this:
We can give birth and run the world.
All at once and in unison.
It blows my mind that we held this down for
millennia and these asshats began to think
about rebelling when we stood upright on the
earth.

Once they grew penises erect and
remembered who was God, they retreated.

It was when they bred our brethren and
called them cattle that they saw the
implications of filling a vessel with their seed.
(Us? Vessels? My, how quickly they forgot)
We are powerful now, they mused.
We can control this place better than them by
force.

And this is why they chose violence.
The power they seek in war and rape
is the orgasm none other can give them.
What silly little boys.
They think us weak for our restraint.
Don't they know the original creator can and
will retake this planet as hers?

The Price We Pay, We Pray

I carry the shame forced into me by my
mother through her mother who birthed the
pain of thousands of us just like me

We didn't do enough to protect ourselves.
It is our fault that it all happened.

So we confess and beat our chest,
mea culpa, mea culpa, mea culpa
Battering our hearts into submission
Folding our bodies into a thousand paper
cranes
The joy that used to radiate a dying ember
And now we have breast cancer from giving
too much
And now our hips are replaced from bearing
the weight of giving them their children and
disposing of our bodies by the side of the
road
Our wombs don't bleed or too much or not
enough or contract with pain
Pain that is ours
Pain that isn't

Slap us with several prescription pills,
they'll never tell us our hysteria is
appropriate

(Why is she anxious?
Why is she depressed?
Why is she so obsessive?

*Why isn't she strong enough to handle all the shit
we do to her with a smile?)*
Perforate the uterus routinely and call us less
than for not opening up on command

*(Take this dick and shut the fuck up.
Let me break you, bitch)*

Hysterectomy, remove our second hearts, and
hope that'll drown us in heat flashes
Bones, hollow and brittle
Cracking, becoming dust under the weight

What's the score now, body?
How much did it cost us to be just a vessel?
Why did you not like it when your death was
first proposed to you?
When did you get ripped out of your dreams
and into his nightmares?
Tell me how you carry their sons and are still
the original sin,
Even when you were and always will be their
redemption.

We didn't do enough to protect ourselves.
It is our fault that it all happened.
They hit us because we were not careful with
their anger
We are clumsy, our small hands like gnats
who need to be swatted dead
Surely, we must be taught.

Dark Versus Light

Yo.
Who or what the fuck is God?

Respectfully and honestly.
Like this entity deadass said, let there be
light.
Aight, first of all, that's lit as fuck.

Darkness called light into being.
And this small piece is always missed.
Entire people would be wiped out in the
name of light. Which is wild to me.

As if to lay waste to the bleak and shadowy
The mysterious and the unknown
That which cannot be measured, quantified,
and not fully comprehended
At least not with the human mind
That which resides in this animal body
The one that can sense and feel long before
the frontal cortex has time to perceive

If darkness is God then ain't light an illusion?

And if God is a dark womb from where all
light and life emerges then wouldn't that
automatically make them androgynous on
account of being both the seed and the
vessel?

Nah I'm trippin'.

But like
Is it plausible that darkness has been painted
as frightening to dissuade an otherwise
curious pilgrim?

It also then occurred to me that God is Black.
Pitch Black.
Blackity black.

The crazy shit though is like
We worship this one life-giving light
The Sun
It's the most relevant star to this tiny ass
planet
(*comparative to...well...an infinite universe*)
And then a whole story was built off the
defeat of darkness

As though darkness did not precede light
As if light has ever conquered darkness

Yo, you know what's crazy?
That these cats think God is a man.

Pero si yo doy luz, entonces quien carajo soy
yo?
If I *give light*, then who the fuck am I?

Sitting here being as dark as I am
I opened up my legs and
Gave all these assholes light

But please, go on about how light (and in
turn, white) is so much more powerful than
darkness
We who rule the shadows
That which cannot be known or seen
Will remind you who lit this shit up and
will shut this shit down

I truly believe we are far too merciful to these
people

But before you get me excommunicated or
some shit like that, I'm just saying.

Isn't the evil committed in the name of light
much more blasphemous than my line of
thinking?

Pleasure/Possession

Sometimes I wonder what I meant to you
If you still kept my picture in your wallet
If you will ever know why I left
If you even care
We painted the bedsheets in our hues of
watercolors
Had we hung our dirty laundry out to dry,
*they may have seen the decadence of our night*s
I had to admit to myself that
I loved you once
In an instant
You were an unraveling thread of temptation
Meant to be spooled just once
Alluring like the scent of body convulsing in
possession
Fucked me guilty like
Saturday afternoon confessionals
Lying you'd never commit the
sin of skin again
You grinned at me from
the shadows of my bedding
and told me that I get religious sometimes when
we pray pelvis to pelvis
I was petitioning for absolution some nights
and other twilight moments,
hoping for an exorcism

A Violent Cupid

There was this arrow aimed at my heart once
Jagged-edged choice of weapon dipped
in the sweetest sin
There I was, bare-chested holding my shirt
open like a Superman wannabe, ready to take
it
Every fiber of my being screaming for mercy
as I shut my eyes and let myself be
penetrated by this foreign metal

No one told me I would bleed so profusely
The blood soaking
My garments as I fell back

My senses weakened as I struggled to breathe
beneath the weight of this decision
To have let you pierce through my armor
You could have told me you planned to cut
deep and contend against the first cut
Could have let me know that there would be
a loud, sickening ripping sound when you
slayed me
There's a hole in my heart, a finger shoved in
deep to stop the flow and stains of my sin all
over my bed

You could have let me know

This
Was
Going

To
Hurt.

Once I pressed my head to your chest and
there was nothing there
Just the sound of the wind howling in the
hollowness
Just the rattle of tin cans on the floor of your
soul
No compassion when you saw how willing I
was to give it all to you
No respect when you didn't bother to ask if
I wanted protection from you

A man like you should wear a warning.
Yet you think you're exempt because you
drew a no-fly zone around your heart and
laced it with the greatest female aphrodisiac
known
Whispering fables that Aesop would
reprimand you for in ears that wanted to hear
That she was wanted
That she was desired

There is nothing innocent about an armed
marksman.

I shackled myself to your memory
Roaming around this earth like your other
victims with fingers shoved deep into the
hole you left
Too scared to let someone else even have a
look

Even though the cut is infected and swollen,
crying out for someone who would be so
gracious as to understand the damage and
teach me
patience with the healing time
You punctured me, and I waited for you to
come back with first-aid

Time passes and you keep me on your mantle
as one of the finest you've hunted
You had your time of conquest
I have my time to heal

As I placed my heart into hands that began to
clean the wound and stitch up your mess
Vowing that the next time I would flinch

Survivor's Report

You women are strong like
black boxes in cockpits
surviving every devastating
crash and explosion
and living to tell the story

The earth asks much of you
giving you a hollow place and a full one
without being able to decipher which
has more grievances

Sometimes you bend over, a body of rubber,
backward to make life easier for them
forwards to please them
sideways to prevent the contact
of a fist or insults
with your pretty little face

At Night

You're always lovelier at night
When the moon kisses your skin
And all I can see is the outline of your body
Smooth like the wine bottles of my deep
infatuation
The faint remnants of cannabis and white
zinfandel
On your lips
Taste like heaven on an unlikely hell
I like your lips when they touch mine;
They're less poisonous that way.

You're so much lovelier at night
So much more innocent and spell binding
I think I fell for the beauty of your silence
The striking conversation in your eyes
And even though tonight everything is
beautiful
I dread the sun because then
Your extraordinary silence becomes empty
And you don't look at me the way you do,
With the sun in your eyes.

Age In Deep With The Seasons

This body has seen the fall and rise of her
earthen breast
The changes in landscape signifying the cycle
of change
Snowy white winters melting into buds on
branch-like fingers
That reach out from the tops of tree trunks to
blossom and be abundant
In the green dew-kissed grass of summer,
under full moons and sudden breezes
That soon become that autumn chill that
yellows the corn and harvests
That which has been reaped
That which was sowed and tended to come to
a silent halt as a winter slumber commences
again
I knew you then

We were once so new
Perennials of the mouth of god
We become so much wiser as each age adds a
layer of past lives and scar tissue to this skin
Feels like the rings counted in the midsection
of a trunk
We age this way
In circles
In cycles
I saw you between the leaves falling from the
canopy decorating the view of
My autumn sky
I learned to look closer

Thought about you as the sun slowly faded
and receded like the ocean waves
Sometimes, the tide is higher because
sometimes the moon is full when I look up to
The sky to understand why everything feels
like it's about to spill over
And then I understand the ebb and flow even
though the influences of each season can be
hard to resign to
Especially in the between when I'm still
reeling from the wine we had over
conversations after the grapes were harvested
and pressed
I know you met me when i was still green
I was a sapling then
As the weather changed, the years are
marked in my aged trunk
As my many hands and arms stretched
forever into the infinite sky above me
I had to be okay with transforming.

A Sick Love

I had your desire wrapped around my finger
and knew how to move to get you to touch
me.
Saying things you wanted to invoke
the incubi in you
just for your attention
Making myself sick just to crack the ice
enough to take a plunge into the iciness
They forget to tell you that fever comes with
chills
Letting you know that something is not right
if you're burning up and freezing too

You had me sick and shuddering
You had me scared and nauseated at
What I settled for
Pieces of you
Pieces of me
Never whole
You had me when I didn't even have myself

Silent Victims

I watch the way the women carry shame in
their bodies;
tiptoeing in the shadows, afraid the sun will
humiliate them.
Faces paralyzed in melancholy, tension
stiffening their necks,
their hips, for fear of one sensual move
anything that may a
waken the beasts who would
leave her for dead and
claim they found her this way.

haikus: unworthy lover

If death bites my lip
when you kiss to convince
my grave is dug in bed.

I will not sleep with
homicidal maniacs
who aim at vulvas.

When Hecate Knew

I swear the lights in the Underworld flickered when he raped Persephone. That's how I knew the Queen had arrived. I felt a surge of ancient power coursing through my veins. The old ones had whispered of her coming, the woman who would tip the scales back into balance. The one who would avenge the deaths and rapes of everyone since the Gods and Titans disrupted the natural order.

Hades had it coming. The entire patriarchy did, for perpetuating and allowing all the atrocities to persist. The Underworld had been our domain, a realm where darkness bowed to our command, where we held sway over the mysteries of the unknown. The goddesses on Mount Olympus were willing and abetting captives of a sick war that ravaged the earth and desecrated the sacred rites of our priestesses.

Her mother lacked the courage of her convictions. Her mother, Demeter, lacked the fierce resolve that should have been her birthright, her spirit broken by generations of patriarchal oppression. Demeter had learned helplessness and how to swallow rage from Rhea and so on, and truly it was the violence of the gods that had stunned her, and them, into forgetting. And it didn't help that Zeus, in his infinite cruelty, had entrusted Hades with the task of maintaining control over the Underworld, using any means necessary to quell dissent.

It was in the bowels of the earth that the Titans had been sent. It was in these caves, caverns, and places that we hid - the Fates, Nemesis, Themes, Medusa, Circe, Metis, Eris, Lilith, Nym, and the Hours. We'd been banished to only be here, the world overrun by men and our power diminished by Hades' iron grip.

And yet, despite the overwhelming despair that threatened to engulf us, we had not been idle. We both counsel the souls dying by the millions and avenge the wrongful deaths being carried out. No one can say we didn't try to fight back; we were overwhelmed by the trail of dead women and children, and countless more shattered lives.

The stench of death hung heavy when I'd roam the earth searching for the other witches, the weight of their suffering bearing down upon me like a crushing weight. I bore witness to so many crimes, that I nearly lost my mind. But even in the darkest of shadows, I found glimmers of hope — women giving birth. I remembered midwifery and how to help women survive at least that.

I knew one day the patriarchy would have its reign thwarted. It was written in the stars and spoken of by the Oracle of Delphi. A woman would be the one to conquer the Underworld and command the fiercest army of goddesses and women to take back what was ours. So when I saw Persephone as a little girl, I had a feeling it would be her. My only regret was that I couldn't do more to protect her from her fate.

Once

I loved you once
Passionately
Desperately
Feverishly
Beneath the disappearing edge of where
spring ended and on the forefront of
summertime
I loved you then
I can still feel your head on my chest
sometimes
Still feel your surrendered breathe shallowly
on me as you fall asleep on me
We came in peace
Left in war
I loved you once
Intimately
The notch on my bed that marks
who you were is distinct
I'll always remember your presence fondly,
like a disease that once defined my existence.

Ungagged

We have pulled the gag from our mouths;
not so quiet like you wish we'd be
no more climbing on top of us,
the violent assault on our bodies
trying to refuse the act our world consented
to;
Now you hear us tell you all the ways you are
Unsatisfying
Distasteful
Disgraceful

This time we will make you
watch us masturbate to orgasm instead
So you can learn a thing or two from our
hands;
We can then successfully show you what you
keep missing in your haste
The way you plunge into things,
like us, like war, like the earth
Digging weapons into things without a
thought about the reverberation of your
actions,
Like your phallus,
Like knives into abdomens,
Like shovels & drills

It's no wonder you never knew the cost:
The pain that sears through us
The cries of families mourning loved ones
The weeping willows lamenting the loss of
more forests

Maybe
If we are all screaming at the top of our lungs,
Naked and bare
You will have to hear all of us
Let yourself go soft,
Unload your gun and
Touch the dirt with the palms of your hands
Lovingly

What She Carries

There are traces of rage engrained deep in
your eyes
They never seem empty but are full of seeing
too much
You try to tuck away this anger, this sinister
stirring of blood red
It is a silent flood that you inherited from
your mother
A contorted twisted mouth open, horrified
that no sounds come out
Choking on the ceramic apple salt shaker that
had been placed neatly by the supper he
never ate

She drowned in the dishwater because she
could never make anything clean enough
Like her mother, who polished her husband's
shoes that complimented the suit she pressed
for him
Feverishly making sure he could see her
where the leather shined in their reflection

Her hands bled from scrubbing his white
shirt collars
Quietly cursing lipstick for its potency
These curses filled her nauseous
Like finding out she had been conceived in
violence
The day your great-grandmother passed the
inheritance the women were expected to
carry

These faces full of bruises,
arms that mend and re-mend
This heart full of aches, of smelling other
women in their beds
Of not being able to distinguish what hair in
the shower was hers
These broken wings from being pulled nearly
in half being assaulted from behind like his
little bitch

Fucked her and called her his whore
Nothing belonged to her, not even her voice
Even the children were not hers

A wounded beast rattled the cage of
her mind viciously scorned
They all did their best to control the
subsequent hysteria with fists, threats, and
pills
Ultimately a hysterectomy

You are one of the lucky ones
The sickness is still close enough to
the surface to be purged
Your tongue is not yet hostage to the
innermost parts of your thorax
The daunting mission to reduce to ashes this
legacy of living chained to these men who
remain blameless in the face of their crimes

Sometimes you look just like your great-
grandmother
Easy to bend back, skin breakable

under the weight of an iron fist
When the light hits you right, you look just
like your grandmother
Pretty
Tiny
Destroyable

But really you are identical to your mother
You hate that
Like a cross you never asked to bear
Lips curling in disgust as the images of her
subordination flood you
If you hadn't already lost so much blood that
night
This mirror would already be shattered

The First Cut Is the Deepest

When you're six, the world should be simple
The hardest dilemma should be trying to
decide whether Santa Claus is real or not
Or who your new best friend will be for the
day
Or even, what game will you choose to
imagine for recess
A game of house is far too complicated to be
considered child's play
When the hardest dilemma for this first-grade
girl is trying to swallow the sickness of
disgust sweeping over her when she is forced
to be a wife

She wanted to say no. the words were stuck
to her like an insect in amber
Desperately wanting to escape but
succumbing eventually to silence
Laying next to a boy that was now her
husband, her stomach convulsed and
spasmed while she forced herself to stay
Her arms becoming leaden when he would
pull her on top of him
Her body a dead weight, lifeless as she
learned how to be a woman, dueling with a
tongue that didn't belong in her mouth

She must have aged 10 years every time they
played until the actions became routine
The young reluctant wife

A lost appetite, her bile digesting her
innocence
She has felt tainted ever since.
And just as quickly as her pseudo-marriage
began, it ended when her instinct kicked in;
She couldn't tell you if she wanted to
The boy had not foreseen this happening,
flinging her on the bed when her lips reached
his neck

It was over.
The earth took her
And swallowed her in that empty bed he left
her on
left to sift through her mind for reasons she
was wrong

She's 14 now and the last of her friends to get
their period
She tells no one that she secretly has believed
God was punishing her for what she did long
ago
And she knows they will look at her with
raised eyebrows if she says that she feels she
has been pregnant for the last 8 years
The show of blood is a sigh of relief;
Maybe she still has a chance at redemption

She's 16 now and her period is sporadic
God must still be mad at her
She's 18 now and in bed with the second man
to ever touch her

The first man who showed her what sex felt
like physically but left so much more to be
desired
She knew she should have never slept with
him; but when you spend so much of your
life feeling like a leper, any bit of attention is
devoured
She lays beside him after they are done and
suddenly She is six again
she whimpers, he holds her as she tells him
What happened
Until it gets to be too much
He tells her to stop crying
The silence falls over her soul
She is six again, forced to swallow her words

She is 20, and a man is looking into her
vagina with a speculum holding her open
She feels this is all wrong but quiets these
thoughts sitting in his office, she tells him she
has an irregular cycle

He tells her she has polycystic ovaries and
that she will have a very hard time having
children
Handing her a prescription for birth control,
he tells her that's all she needs to be normal
All she remembers is the feeling of her chest
imploding
they took my innocence and now my babies
God, you really do hate me. I really am
broken.

She is 24 and is still scared she is broken
I am 24, and I am still scared I don't function
the right way
She still thinks I did something to mess up
my ovaries
I wonder when this absolution will ever come
When life will regain the simplicity I could
never enjoy
This is the sadness I've carry
This is my deepest wound.

Adonis

Little boys also get violated.
I know this because
Some of those little boys grew up and
became the men I slept with
A topic of pillow talk
I've heard so many stories
Caught tears that had been held in too long
After the closest they can come to intimacy
with another person;
The only kind that is permissible for them
It is then that they disclose
Having kept that secret their whole lives
And when I named the crime for what it was
They'd stiffen and close up
Often denying that it was assault
Instead, naming it as their initiation into
manhood

Their mothers aided and abetted the
patriarchy to destroy their childhood
Circumcising them unceremoniously was
their first act of violence
(So they can look like their fathers)
Hastily silencing their cries and any emotion
the boys dared to show
Big boys don't cry
Crushing any sign that would signal
femininity
Man up
Seen as little men instead of children,

they are left defenseless against the
patriarchy
Defenseless against babysitters, aunts,
fathers, uncles, teachers, coaches, and other
trusted adults
Even the mothers themselves crossed the line
To later join the ranks of the ones who abused
them and continue the cycle
Repetition compulsion
Tender hearts turned to stone, locking all
feeling away to emulate the patriarchs

Aphrodite cried at the altar of the patriarchy
for Ares
Forced into a loveless marriage with
Hephaestus, the only things she had to show
for it were the bruises she covered up with
her makeup
She was humiliated and degraded yet hated
for her beauty
When the adoration from everyone couldn't
drown out her bitter cries for love
She acquired a taste for war and ran her
tongue down Ares' sword
Enjoying the familiar metallic taste in her
mouth
And when that wasn't enough, the thrill of
waging it on another aroused her

When she found Adonis, he was still a boy
Handsome and tall with a baby face
How she was filled with lust for him was
despicable

She thought herself above reproach
She had to have him
And besides, who cares what happens to little
boys?
Certainly not the head rapist in charge, who
had young Ganymede as his personal
cupbearer and sex slave
Because raping the shit out of women wasn't
enough for him, he had to permanently fuck
a little boy into submission

Adonis was a mere mortal who was caught in
an awful web of perversion
It was Persephone with whom he reenacted
what he learned from Aphrodite
Causing her harm when her younger body
reacted to him and pushed her away
So many are harmed when adults cross the
line

Little boys don't matter as long as they
become men who cannot cry
Men who cannot remember they were
violated
Men who will go ahead and rape other little
boys and initiate them
Men who will break women in half and eat
their insides and then force them to be their
mothers
Consequently taking out their rage on them

Who cries for the little boys?

Who should have sobbed for Adonis the way
Aphrodite did?
God save the little boys who are killed long
before their natural deaths
May the patriarchy choke on their young
Have mercy
My god

For the Leaping Tongues of Fire Women
(Psalm of Artemis)

You think beauty such as this is fragile,
delicate, and in need of your big hands
Hands to cover, cradle, and protect the
compromised state you seem to have
assumed of me

Beauty like mine is none of these
I am leaping tongue of fire blinding beauty
Astoundingly awe-inspiring with ferocity

You think me weak little womanly thing
To bend me back to break me
So beautiful you must destroy it

What? With your ghastly brute strength?
Strapping muscled force?
There is nothing delicate about your scent
Musk of violence, simply out to destroy
everything you touch

Could you be awe-struck again and touch me
curiously?
Touch my skin with your lips to taste me,
Saving teeth for something more suitable to
crush in your jaws

Could you remember, eyes shut
The veneration of your mother
She was once dancing dandelion
Woman of joy and rapture

Made beautiful, forged by fire and flame
Force and resistance
I can smell the perfume of her sex on
Your skin, amniotic fluid scented
Could you remember the way momma
rubbed her belly?
"I could never break you."

I hope you remember when I give myself to
you
That you take no prisoner or ruins of war
This is no leaky faucet for you to plug up
I did not come here for you to save me.

Reduce yourself; shrink back to a human
having a connection with another human
being
I have survived death in ways you will never
have to think of contriving
Having ingested hemlock-laced violations
that wanted to kill me

Is this why you cannot fathom discussing the
uncomfortable?
That you assume to know the sutures to
wounds you've never studied?
You're so used to sleeping with corpses
How about you try surviving making love to
a woman full of life
Making your physical knowledge useless
Asking you to understand this place I am
taking us to
Asking you to stop doing sex like it's a favor

Asking you to trace the scars on me
So you can understand how well I heal.

Man of conquest
Boy accustomed to melting toy soldiers
There is nothing here to murder
There is too much fertile here
My legs rooted deep in the ground I grow
from

I suppose you are used to being sand
Getting into everything and everywhere
Filling empty spaces

I am impermeable
I will only let you visit
Come hither and recognize I am woman
Whole
Complete
Capable of falling apart
Just to come together improved and better

Without you.

For the Men (and Women) Who Forgot

When did you, for one moment, deem it okay
to bring war into this bed?
My dreams, conjured in these pillows
My strife, diffused under my covers
This peace in my chest, I open to you

In this lifetime of struggle
When did you forget?

You smell of ashes and gunpowder
Blackened sweat from all the others you've
combusted
I do not understand how to divorce love from
sex
If this is the place we began
As you aim your weapon into my hallowed
womb
I dare ask
When did I become a foxhole to detonate
explosives in?

Let me tell you something.
Your mother was me once
She was once this vulnerable, this ready to
accept the natural progression of her
womanhood
We inherited a history so cold, so destructive
That we come from generations of women
who forgot

Forgot the primordial womb from where all
life was begotten
That a male fetus must emit as much
testosterone as possible to survive a woman's
body
That not only is a clitoris an underdeveloped
penis but a penis is an overdeveloped clitoris
That we have numbers and calendars because
women have a reason to count
That women not only give birth to
civilization but it is because of us that culture
and society even exist

We forgot
We are the inventors of basic life industries -
cooking, food processing, ceramics, weaving,
the medicinal arts
Language
We first discovered how to use and produce
fire, known in legends as the owners of it

She, like me, forgot herstory.

When you fell one day
When you ran too quickly, fell, and scraped
your knees
Was she not there to clean you and kiss the
wound?
And you believed she could work magic
That belief alone healed the sting
She was your hero

How could you?

How could you be so heartless, blinded by
the patriarchy that encourages your amnesia?
How could you forget my body is not a
battlefield?
How could you have the audacity to forget
your sisters, daughters, and cousins?

How
Could
You
Forget
Your
Mother?

Reflection

I don't know if I am strong enough to be this
vulnerable
With my tendency to run with the wind when
I consider you

You forgive the way plants push through
once hardened soil to be in plenty again
I am quiet like a land blanketed by snow

When I think of what I lost
I question why I left it
So openly
In the lines of your hands

They tell me I am still whole
I know it is because I could not carry
everything of the pieces I made
Like an oak tree mourning her leaves crushed
and crumbled beneath the weight of being
ephemeral
You were the end of autumn, a harvest of the
things we planted in each other
Just to see what would come of it

Is my memory laminated and plastic, to never
know the ways time ages us into wisdom?
Or am I a grainy, faded photograph full of
every night you stared at it
Holding it with your fingers, letting your
prints embed themselves in me

All the age was instigated by you; you
couldn't help yourself

I push myself wide open to find the answer
again
Wrestling with regret that threatens to fasten
all the exit wounds on my body shut so that
your voice could never leave me
Because I cannot be a thousand lifetimes of
winter, scared to give spring a chance
When summer beats in my chest, wanting to
know the abandon of heat again

Accountability

If you did not want
To get so deep
To be clutched tightly
And slip, and be drenched
In my plentiful waters
You should have not cum here

Aphrodite, Goddess of Beauty
(The Beautiful Whore)

She was the baddest bitch on Mount Olympus. And Aphrodite knew it. She was the goddess of love, beauty, and pleasure. She was born of the sea foam after Cronus castrated his father Uranus and threw the penis into the ocean, which makes sense considering how she was so good with cocks and knew what to do with them.

Aphrodite was a sight to behold. She had smooth milky white skin, a gorgeous bone structure, and bouncy golden ringlets down her back with an hourglass figure. Everyone wanted her, especially Ares. Her laughter was enchanting, her face beat to the gods, and her robes were always shades of pink and red. It's actually a miracle Zeus never tried to tap that ass.

The most unfortunate part of her life was her forced marriage to Hephaestus, the god of blacksmiths and fire. He was a hard worker and very skilled at his work, but definitely not considered handsome by any stretch of the imagination. Not compared to Ares, the papi chulo of her heart.

Alas, Zeus made Aphrodite marry Hephaestus to avoid all the gods fighting to death over her. That didn't necessarily stop Aphrodite from doing her.

She had a number of lovers but her favorite was Ares. Aphrodite fucked Ares whenever she got the chance. Dique Hephaestus was the best choice for husband because he wasn't jealous but the dude once made an unbreakable iron net to catch them in the act. He laid it over her bed and when they were in mid-fuck, caught them in it and dangled them in the main hall of the palace so everyone could see them. Interestingly enough though, Hephaestus made Aphrodite's famous girdle which made her irresistible to men; the math here is not mathing at all.

Por más linda que era, no one knew or cared about how thick her makeup was on her face. I was curious though. At the mouth of Styx, I saw her in the water. I'm not sure if it was a mirage or if she was actually there but it took me a few seconds until I recognized her.

Aphrodite was before her vanity table but she was unlike herself. Her face was bruised and her lip was split as silent tears streamed down her face. I was aghast, as I had never seen her without makeup and certainly not this way. She was wiping her face and tenderly touching her wounds, wincing from the pain. Who did this to her?

"*La mujer que tiene todo.* The woman who supposedly has everything," she said to her reflection spitefully. The anger twisted her face for a moment before breaking into a wide-tooth smile.

"I must be more careful. Hephaestus and Ares should not be bothered when they are angry. I am so stupid and clumsy," she said in a high-pitch voice. She began to laugh as she picked up a make-up brush. The foundation began to slowly erase the marks on her. Aphrodite's laughter got louder and more desperate until suddenly she looked at herself again. She burst into tears, slapped herself hard, and gave her reflection the best smile.

"At least Adonis loved me," she said again in that high-pitch voice. "Poor Myrrah. I would have gagged if I fucked my daddy," Aphrodite giggled, "No one will ever know I bewitched that stupid bitch into such a disgusting deed for not being loyal to me." Her face darkened, eyes welling up with tears again. "He was such a beautiful little boy," she whimpered. "I was like his mother but better and more rewarding."

A wail escaped her throat as she screamed his name. "Adonis! Why did you leave me?!" As sudden as her outburst was, she stopped herself and picked up her powdered foundation.

Aphrodite was sitting there naked and I noticed the rest of her body was covered in blacks and blues. Must be love marks. With her face beaten to the gods again, she dressed herself and stood up. Smoothing her hair over and checking her makeup one more time, she walked away.

For the Would-Be Pendejas

1.
Parted thighs like two sides of a valley
How I forgot something once lived in
between
There was once an insatiable thirst for every
drop of you
Not knowing how to love the hollow parts of
me
Craving anything, even if it was not fit for
this body
For this soul
For this woman.
In the thoughts crossing my mind in the
silence of your absence, I realize empty
spaces need not always be filled.

2.
Nausea overcomes me as I remember how
much was endured by women before me
Just for me to spit in their faces
Reducing their struggle to give value to the
disintegrated feminine mystique
To making sure his wandering eyes found
repose on the slithering of my body
Desperation is a selfish motherfucker.
Making every burned bra
Every rally for sexual freedom
Every fight for equality
Every word bell hooks, Patricia Smith, Assata
Shakur, and my mother uttered

Another sickening feast for a patriarchal
juggernaut.

3.
If that nigga told you he was fucking you,
your friend, and the next bitch
There is
Without a shadow of a doubt
An overwhelming conclusion
That you were acting like a pendeja
You should be offended.
Fuck that
Your pussy should be offended
That your lack of integrity had the audacity
to
Put to shame all the work you put into her
She didn't get
That tight
That wet
That talented
For nothing.

4.
Queens who act like slaves
Walk the streets of the city
I joined their ranks
Tarnishing my crown with every lie
Every night he was allowed to reduce me to a
peasant
A lovely piece of rubbish
Today
I go shopping
Sparkling tiara

Flowing white dress
Flowers in my hair
Diamond encrusted sandals
Brand new self-esteem.

Her Truth

What about the women who can't even bring themselves to use the word?
The ones who can't fit in their brains what happened to them, some people call it *rape*.
What of the women who have to show up to the rally and the meeting and work right alongside the Huey Newton (Che, Malcolm X, Albizu, etc) wannabe who forced himself inside her?
What of the women who believed his politics would match his morals?

What of the women emotionally and mentally violated?
What of the married women who are forced to have sex by their husbands and are invisible on the abuse spectrum?
What of the woman who will never talk about what happened because a part of her believes she deserved it, that she should have known better?
What of the woman who sees how much our views of sexual assault forces many women into silence because there was no Special Victim's Unit, rape kit, cuts, bruises or jury to validate that they were just ripped apart from the inside?

What of them?
What of me?
What of she?

What of the guilt and shame we women carry?
What of the woman who purposely avoids certain situations, locations, neighborhoods, and events because she is scared to see him?
What of the woman who wants to shout from the rooftops how much pain she's in, who he was, and how he did it and is crippled by the fear that he might pin her down again and fuck her to punish her?
What about working up the guts to face him, only to find out he has no recollection at all about what he did to her?
What about this woman, who feels like her entire body is a jagged wound every time she tries to get close to another man?

What about the violence of the silence?
Of the cry caught in her throat, the pain in her chest, and the fury in her womb?
What of the women who can't call it rape but have decided that they have no clue what the fuck happened? That all they know is that something happened that fucked them up?

She speaks in private, behind closed doors, so as to not expose the truth.
She cries sometimes, or not at all.
She cringes.
She can still feel him on top of her.
She is still recovering.
She knows, painfully and angrily, that she is not the first and unfortunately not the last.

Puerto Rico

She loved Puerto Rico so much, she made
love to him.
Couldn't get enough, she stayed on that
vacation for far too long
It was a childhood infatuation
An innocent fascination with a place she
never saw

Met him in a cloud
Of the finest herb that could have been
inhaled that night
He saw what he wanted
She was all too enthralled
He smelled like salt and ocean
Sweat and work
Blunts and beers
Skilled hunter, trained to capture even
the wildest of prey
Skilled at plotting the best way to hit his
mark squarely
Between the legs

He was fluent in English, Spanish, and
Cunnilingus
He got up in her
All up in her
*(He did ask if he could though; hard to say no
when he's halfway there.)*

Had her speaking in tongues
Had her dripping, slippery enough just to

slide in easily
Had her screaming his name,
"Puerto Rico! Ohhhh!"
Had her ready to give it all up.

It was a vision of blue Caribbean Sea
Often dreamt of this warmth, this heat
To open her skin up to this gluttonous
obsession
With his landscape
With his waves crashing into her coastlines

Never been plucked this way
Never knew how empty she was until he
tried to fill her
With his sand getting into every space she
had
With his hands becoming keepers of her skin
She loved Puerto Rico. Too damn much.
His swagger
His scent
The way sex oozed from every single pore on
His body
Oh god.
His body.
His chiseled physique
His perfectly tan, butter pecan skin
His endowment
(*The man was very well endowed, goodness
gracious!*)
A healthy set of family jewels

Slayed by the penis
Dickmatized, so to speak
His words, fashioned only to get her where
he wanted her
She ignored everything he didn't say
Knew too early there was no love, only greed
(Ese degraciao!)
Instead of saying, "I'm just one of his hoes."
Becoming, "One of his choices."

(Like that shit sounds better.)
Like saying commonwealth
Instead of colony
Controlled and used
Never replenished
Robbed of its true riches

Love and lust
Are not the same
Lied too long to herself
Realizing she needed to unbound herself
Seek self-determination

Lose the shackles of the lies she believe
For a lesson in independence she never
foresaw
Washed up back on her land
Back to reality
To the truth that she was simply infatuated
Almost fatally
She loved Puerto Rico so damn much,
she let him fuck her.
And he did. Because he could.

Almost

I lived to be the ecstasy in your ear
Grazing the crevices of your bodyscape
Majestic peaks of perfectly sculpted mounds
Gently rolling into the valleys of your hips

I lived to touch you there
So you could contest with
the stillness of my walls
That hadn't felt the quake of life in years

I almost felt special as
I watched you disappear into dreamland,
Your once rhythmic body
motionless among my sheets

I almost felt important that you laid
Your post-coitus vessel to rest
Instead of making haste with the wind

Almost

Until I found the map to my body composed
A collage of scraps from other anatomies
A skill to be mastered
Another land to be conquered

El Enfermo

Él era enfermo con las mujeres.
A raging sickness of obsession with plunging
into and pulling out of women who bared
themselves naked and vulnerable to him time
and time again.
He moved through the crowd, searching for
his prey. Searching for the hostess who would
willingly surrender herself to
this parasite in disguise.
And he would stop short and stare intently at
the one before him. A dancer, gyrating her
hips vividly, almost thrashing like wire,
flagellating water hose.
Her scent filling his nostrils as the sweat flew
off her, whirling skirt, wild hair.
Lilith in the flesh.
He, Adam, wanting her to ride him.
He imagines her lively rhythmic body
horizontal, beneath him.
Finally conquered.
Taking advantage of an impassioned woman,
made wet by innuendo, intellectual foreplay,
and several sangrias. Each stroke hitting her
deeper inside, his victory signaled by each
orgasm resonating in her soul, clenching
tightly around his endowment in hopes that
somehow she could keep him there forever.

La Enferma

_Ella amaba con sus piernas abiertas y su corazón
zafándose por allí._
It was much easier than real conversation and
less scarier than being honest.
She thought love meant a high, taking hits of
it to feel its effects and always found herself
in the depth of shattered illusions.
Left hungry, practically starving, she needed
something to feed the insatiable appetite of
her pussy, her second heart.
She beckoned all the hims that only wanted
the pleasure of her heat with her hips,
dancing desperately the way strippers work
for their singles but with less dignity.
And when, countless condoms later, she had
nothing to show for the fantasies turned
nightmares, she tried on the violence of being
hunted.
Naked and compromised, she surrendered
her body as a host for any leech of a man to
feast and suck dry.
And she, with the inability to see how rotten
and dangerous her need to be filled was, kept
lying to herself about him and what he really
wanted in the raw, so deep.

The Love of My Life, Hades

Do you know what it's like to be in love with
a god?
Time and space bend in brief moments of
endless erotic passion.
When our bodies press against each other,
our souls become ecstatic.
Every past life moves itself between forces of
nature.

He was the love of my life.
I was deeply and madly in love with him.
I was obsessed with him.
I was obsessed with the idea of him.
I was addicted to the way he made my body
feel.
I could see all of our children when
my eyes rolled back in pleasure.

A god only loves the idea of us and the
ecstasy of our flesh.
So much so that they will resort to the worst
of crimes - to deceive the one that loves them,
feverish as it may be, for access to their body
or to take them by force.

Never look at them in the eyes.
They will take the last of what remains of
your mortal soul and discard you.

I locked myself in a watery tomb and let the
river rush into my lungs

I didn't want to feel any of the love that
I had for him.

A deep shame of who I was with him made
me shut my eyes forever to myself.
I drowned every sob, and every scream
The screams trapped in my throat
when he ripped me apart

River Styx couldn't kill me fast enough even
as I swallowed furiously to hasten my death

I'd sooner stuff my clothing with rocks and
Walk into the water with the heaviest stone I
could hug
All I knew was that I was dead.
All I knew was that I hated myself.
All I knew is that I wanted to forget.

Waiting in the Kitchen

I am blown, scattered, a mess each time you, misguided love, come through my front door.

Every time, I waited for you in my kitchen, cutting onions and damping the counter with fallen promises of something real. I was making dinner. Always making you something to eat, hoping you would stop feasting on the inside of my thighs. So that I might watch you ravenously tear into the steak I always wanted to serve you. So that I may know what you look like when you want something to fill you. I knew I could never.

It is your reluctance to face me after you've gotten off (in, on…) me. It is your rejection of a carefully brewed cup of coffee, as though mine wasn't good enough for you. It is all these things that told me a long time ago that I gave you too much.

I've thought of the way the knife might draw blood from your neck if I pressed hard enough. My only consolation is wiping the juices off the counter from the chicken I prepare for myself, in an attempt to placate my starvation. It never seems to be enough. I don't seem to be enough. You are insulting; searching for something else to eat in my refrigerator without permission. My body placed neatly on a silver platter, my heart as dessert, and still, you rummage for leftovers.

You make such few sounds, outside of the ones you utter when you're enjoying being in the middle of me. I drown them out as I wash the dishes while you roll out of my bed. My body always cringes when you slam the door on your way out, out of fear that this house is not strong enough to support such a blow. And silently, as I turn on the stove to boil water for my cup of tea, I pray that if this place should collapse, let it be when I finally step outside. Let it be when I finally have the strength to drop this knife, remove this apron and walk out on your sleeping corpse; you always seemed dead to me anyways.

What Killed Virginia Woolf?

Sometimes I close my eyes
and imagine being at the
bottom of the river.
The feeling evoked in my
body is one of profound peace.

When they told me how
they found Virginia Woolf
with no signs of homicide
washed up on the shore,
the hair at the nape of my
neck stood on end
Mentally ill, they said
With an aversion to men
I wonder if the sexual abuse
made her crazy too

I wonder how much peace
the sight of the river gave her
 and how often she
imagined herself freed of
her memories of the water
Letting go of the pain and
giving it to the one that can
hold it all
Some of us know better than to go visit
alone at night when reality
is too painful

Dear Patriarchy:

You have maimed my brothers by caging their emotions inside them and feeding aggression on a gluttonous diet. We, women, suffer from too much; the men suffer from too little. No space to cry, to love, to embrace their softness, to be vulnerable. You taught them to negate any notion that they are anything less than suffocatingly masculine with violence. I feel sometimes they are just as paralyzed as the women. I weep for the little boys who were told to stop. I hold the men who still can.

Dear Patriarchy:

You have taught my sisters and I that we must move our words around in our mouths. Swish them to make them gentle, filter out anything that may be offensive, that may cause a backhand to strike me in the mouth. I am not your mother. Not all my words will be dipped in sugar for you to swallow easily. In fact, you will probably gag when the women untie their tongues.

Dear Patriarchy:

I gave you too much rope to hang yourself
with.
I have complied with my silence.
I have murdered my own sisters for you.
I sent so many to burn at the stake and
watched idly as you tortured them.

I helped to numb you. I told you to stop
crying and man up. I questioned your
masculinity when you would show emotion.

I told you those belonged to me only.
I remained dangerously neutral when you
denied that there ever was a rape.
Several of them.
Matter of fact, innumerable.

I acquiesced to your demands.
I never put you on trial.
I have been scared for too many millennia.
I was afraid you would kill me with your
bare hands.
I let myself be defined by you.
I made too many excuses for your
thoughtless maniacal violence.
I still don't understand how you could dare
blame me for my femininity.

I don't know why I believed you for so long.
Why did I let you mispronounce my name,
later forgetting it?

Dear Patriarchy:

There is this need to communicate with you that I cannot placate. It doesn't make sense. Why would the prey put herself so close to the predator? Why would the plaintiff keep pleading with the defendant?

It is this sick twisted love I have for you. Because you came from me. Because you cannot exist without me, and I cannot exist without you. Because I helped create you and cannot stand here blameless while you run rampant destroying everything you touch.

I must be some masochistic abused lover who likes to be beaten repeatedly by you. It must be the mother in me who keeps her arms open for her prodigal son, even though he spat in her face and kicked her when she was down.

More than angry and disgusted with you, which are two emotions that color my perception of you, I feel sorry for you. I am overwhelmed with pity. It is sad to watch you self-destruct, and painful to be taken down with you.

All I wanted was your attention. My father went AWOL years before I was born. I just wanted you to love me. That's why I keep throwing myself at you, since my vulva seems to be your favorite plaything and you have ripped out my eyes, gagged me voiceless, and denied my right to be alive.

You asked me the other day why I won't answer to "bitch" anymore. I must remind you that you have stolen my heat and I am too cold to warm myself. And you no longer deserve anything from me, as much as it hurts me to withhold it.

These letters are a warning, not a plea. I struggle constantly with the demons you sent to haunt me as I muster the strength to leave the dungeon you shackled me in. I can no longer give birth to any more of your godforsaken sons. My womb cannot handle any more of your evil.

That's why I won't answer to "whore" anymore. I am staring out at the ocean contemplating my return to where we both came from. This letter is not a threat. This letter is your death sentence. A call for your return to your sanity. A list of grievances that call for both of us to make amends; you have a much taller order than I.
You are no longer welcome in my bed. Stay away from my daughters. Throw yourself at the feet of my sisters. Serve at the coronation of my mothers. You are a beast that must be kept in isolation, for the damage you have created is unforgivable.

The Savior

It is written that Jesus conquered Satan when
he died for three days and
came back from the dead.
I'd like you to say that shit with a straight
face to every single person who has ever
given birth and will give birth.
That it was Jesus and
Jesus alone who conquered death.

That this man on the cross did more for
humanity than the millions who've died
birthing the next generation.
That the ultimate sacrifice is made daily to
allow life a chance to survive.
It is often a miracle that everyone comes out
alive on the other side.

Is it not evil how they try to kill us when we
are allowing life to come through us?
Who, then, truly has saved us and continues
to deliver us from evil?

At the risk of sounding blasphemous,
I've given birth;
I have gotten a glimpse of salvation for this
godforsaken world and it does not look like
Jesus coming back.
No. It's the ones who've stayed and
kept this shit going.

Switchblade

Women like me have
Switchblade tongues
Ready to strike even without
Provocation.
We know this.
We want to be soft.
Replace it with
A butter knife;
Be less severe,
Less deadly.
Our mouths carry the wounds
Of our own sharpness.
We've been trying to survive
Being so delicate;
It is hard to discern
When to disarm.

For The Woman Who
Refuses to be Broken In

You ask me why I cannot be still
Why this is just the calm before the storm
There is vinegar in me waiting for baking
soda
To cause everything to spill over

You asked me once if there was ever a time in
my life
That I wanted to just be tame
If I was ever anything other than a wild thing
Who kept a bit in her mouth long enough to
be ridden safely

I was told that all I needed was to be broken
in
Tried on and walked around in, a pair of
leather shoes
Something to be molded around another
body
I was told
I had duties, a cloud whose only purpose was
to rain
Instead of holding heaviness too
uncomfortable to be discussed
That I needed to know my place
as the one with the wound that bleeds
Just so you know I can still be filled with your
inheritance
You want to count each coin,
each nickel pouring from me

Manners must be perfect
And I must always be gracious, forgiving,
and kind
Like your mother

Boy
I am not your mother
I am still that quiet tempest you met
Needing to clench the muscles in my eyes to
prevent from flooding all over you
I am not your towel that you can wipe your
hands all over
And just be left to lay there

It is not easy to be a wild thing
I am in constant revolt with myself
And you are not helping by wanting to
straddle me and own me
I am
Fickle
Limber
Supple body
Legs of oak
Elegant in my element of huntress

Domesticate another animal
Another one more submissive than
I am ever willing to be
And ask yourself
Did you want a woman?
Or did you want to be a master?

Grieving

They say the only constant thing is change
I've always been curious why
the other constant thing is excluded
Loss has been my unwanted permanent
companion in this life

I'm getting quite good at grief;
I've stopped resisting the quiet chair in the
dark corner where
I go to feel the weight of the things that have
died
I've stopped expecting grief to be less biting
or less sharp when it renews itself and
stretches into my soul

A body exhausted from sorrow
Opens itself up again to feel the inevitable
And it is almost comforting to know that
I grieve so profoundly because
I loved things that change constantly

In the mourning
I weep for the sun that will only stay but so
long
The warmth of day that will be gone too soon
Emptying myself and losing
With everything to gain

Bruja's Tragedy (After Hozier)

He said, _"Babe, there's something so tragic about you. Something so magic about you. Don't you agree?"_

There are pieces of beauty within the
decomposing material of this thing
I call my life

Ashes of what we wanted to stay permanent
When they come looking for my body, they
will find a circle cast and candles burned
down to a wasteland of wax and wick

When they ask you, tell them to make magic
of the tragic is not for the weak;
The way life reckons me twist a knife into it
Is the way that same life asked me to scream
in such a way that would leave a mark.

There was joy, rage, happiness, and pain
And I couldn't hide the parts they wanted
silenced
So I ran to the woods to shout incantations
They said there was a magic about me
And that it would shine if I wasn't such a sad
girl

What of the moment of birth?
Such agony replaced by the joy of new life

The quiet fear that comes with knowing
you're about to lose everything and the
lightness of that freedom
My contentment is tinged with the grief most
pretend isn't there

My resistance to their epithets is retorting and
spilling all the ancient madness, wit, wisdom,
and awe that made them burn the ones like
me alive

(Monsters. All of them.
Try them all for treason.
They call me crazy so they never need to admit
How they loved her and ripped her out from me.
And how angry they were that she would dare to
defy even death.
What sorcery is this?)

I said, "Baby, life is a juxtaposition of
nightmares and daydreams.
I hope you don't flinch when
I show you how that lives inside me"

Who I Am

When the woman that comes out of my
mouth is the woman I've wanted to be
Something inside me
Like the remnants of patriarchy
Shakes in fear
That I really am that powerful
If left undisturbed and untamed
I could take out an entire system
I realize that I used to say I was sorry so often
So someone wouldn't make me sorry
In fear
That the honesty would anger someone with
an iron fist
Bloodied or not, the truth is mine to speak
So when the woman that needs to
Come out of my mouth
Says her piece
What is left in the deafening silence
Is the voices of the women killed
Before they could get the words out
"You finna' git yourself kilt fo' what you be
sayin, chile."
They will kill me either way.
At least let me go out screaming.

Hecate, My Midwife

I called out to God. To the goodness and
merciful in this godforsaken place. For pity.
For help. For salvation.

I'd learn later that I was the God I sought.

I didn't realize I was carrying life inside me
until I felt a sharp pain like no other rip
through my body. Looking down, I was
horrified at how round and bloated I'd
become. I shut my eyes as I slumped against
the wall of some cavern when another pain
took the wind out of me. _How could I feel
anything if I was dead?_

The next pain I felt, I could not hold back a
scream. I thought I was going to die again
from the pain. It hit me too late that I was
going to need help. _But who was going to help
me? No one can hear me._

It was as though some monster or creature
wanted to split me apart from inside. I felt
myself losing the ability to stand and keep
my eyes closed. The last thing I saw was a
dark figure moving towards me.

When I came to, I was naked in water.
Something in the shadows moved towards
me.

"Who are you?" My voice was trembling from fear and the renewed awareness of pain.

"Hecate. One of the oldest witches and midwives."

Hecate moved towards me with some warmth steaming from the clay bowl. I could see the shadow of wrinkles that had collected themselves by the corners of her almond-shaped sage eyes with the faint light from her hearth. Dark brown curls framed her round face and high cheekbones. Her mouth was red and the shape of a heart. Her face was a kindness I'd forgotten existed in this world. My chest and arms were draped over the side of the tub, my belly and the rest of my body submerged in waters from Mnemosyne.

She looked over at me as my body came to life, my eyes meeting hers with agony.

"It hurts to become," I said through gritted teeth.

Lifting her shirt to show me the deeply etched stretch marks in the skin hugging her abdomen, she takes in a solemn breath with her eyes closed.

"I know, Persephone. I know."

"Why is this taking so long?" I growled as my uterus contracted. It was so painful. It had been a long time since I felt anything at all resembling life in my body.

"This is the way we have given birth for millennia."

I did not want to feel. I spent countless years avoiding my body, floating above it, and going through the motions in darkness. This creature in my womb was demanding I give them light. This birth required me to open up and let them go. I barely even registered that I was pregnant this whole time. I didn't want to have something else of his in my body.

Hecate could only do so much to help me. I had to do the work. Truth be told, I did not want to have the children of Hades. I wanted to die but these beings were forcing me to come back to life.

We stayed like this for four days. I wailed and screamed, praying we would all die and never make it to the other side. Until hours before they were born, Hecate came in and sat in front of me.

"What is it, my child? Why do you want to die? Why do you want to kill your baby?"

I turned away, not wanting to speak. Not wanting to cry. Not wanting to let go.

"You will be in labor forever if you don't give birth. There is no more death for a dead woman like you."

A single tear escaped my eye.

"He raped me."

Hecate had her back to me. Her entire body stiffened when the words left my mouth. She turned around with rage in her eyes.

"HE DID WHAT?!"

I let more tears fall, from her reaction and from the pain ripping through me. No one had ever, to my knowledge, shown any shred of anger towards something that had happened to me.

Hecate took a deep breath to get her bearings, got close to me, and cupped my face.

"I want you to hear me, child. It was not your fault."

I looked down and shut my eyes.

"I should have never drank so much."

"No. He should have never touched you. Do you hear me? He was wrong."

I let myself go limp with tears that I couldn't stop. Hecate held me as I let go. I have never before felt so safe and held in the arms of someone. It was the most relief I've ever had in my whole life, to completely collapse and relax my entire body in her embrace. To be held. To have someone carry my weight, even for a moment. Suddenly, my contractions got longer and closer together. I squeezed my eyes shut and prayed.

Then I started screaming at the top of my lungs and banged my fist on the side of the tub.

"I CAN'T DO THIS! I CAN'T DO THIS!!!"

Hecate smiled. "You're doing it."

I could feel every muscle in my body on fire. I could feel my body again as I was forced to reckon with its power. My hips were in motion, bones shifting and unlocking to release the children I could barely understand wanted me to be their mother.

I reached between my legs with great trepidation as I clenched my jaw. Scared by what I might find there, I moved away quickly as another contraction ripped through me.

"Breathe, Persephone. Loosen your jaw and let yourself feel."

I tried to surrender but desperately wanted to stop the immense pressure that made me feel more like I was about to have a massive bowel movement. Hecate had been giving me space but came up close. She placed her hands on my shoulders, which were tensed and nearly up to my ears at this point, and firmly but gently pushed on them.

"Breathe, Persephone. Let go of the tension. You are safe. I am here with you."

I began softening while I had a break from my uterus squeezing. Without thinking, I closed my eyes and took a deep breath. It was then that I let myself feel and relax with Hecate's hands gently on my back. I reached between my legs again and nearly pulled away, but my utter fascination at what I felt overpowered my fear.

I felt hair in my fingers and it suddenly dawned on me that my hand was touching the little bit of head that was starting to emerge. I began to cry as an immense amount of love and grief came over me. I had a choice. Either crush this head with my thighs or let them pass.

On the next contraction, I felt an uncontrollable urge to push. I felt more of the head come out, and my body kept pushing until a small body came out of me and into the water. I was mesmerized and stunned. Not long after, my hand felt yet another head and another baby emerged as Hecate was just taking the first one out and drying it. Finally, my body had one last set of contractions. I can't remember the pain; I was awe-struck watching the last child leave my body. Three of them.

They were magnificent creatures. I felt euphoric, a strange sense of pride washing over me for the work I had done. Hecate got me out of the water as I remained in a daze. She placed me in the bed near us and as I recovered my senses, she put the three babies in my bed.

I was suddenly repulsed by them and wanted to push them away. I wanted to push my memories of what happened to me away. *Why did I have to go through all of that?* I turned my back to Hecate and shut my eyes so that I wouldn't see them.

I heard my children crying but the sound seemed distant. I felt Hecate take them away and someone else took them. She sat beside me and we were in silence for what felt like forever. I fell into a deep sleep.

When I woke up, Hecate was still beside me. I turned to her and immediately burst into tears. I began to tell her everything that had ever happened to me. I told her about my mother and how she didn't seem to be there at all. Adonis and making him disgusted with me. My father and the stories I had heard. Hera and how much she hated me and my mother. And Hades. How he was the only man who had ever given me attention and how madly I fell in love in an instant. And I cried even harder as I told her that I wanted to kill myself and my children by walking back into the river. I wanted so desperately to forget. After I fell silent, she gave me a warm cup of tea. Hecate stood up and left momentarily. She came back with some towels and a plate of food. Before giving me my first postpartum meal, she checked between my legs to see how much I was bleeding.

I remained silent as I thought about my children. I couldn't kill them. The thought was horrifying. *How can I love them when they come from him?* I sat there and ate quietly as I thought about this.

"Maybe you would like to see them?" Hecate asked, startling me out of my thoughts. My eyes welled up again.

"How long have I been asleep?"

"About seven days."

I was taken aback. I knew I'd have to face them eventually. I felt torn but somewhere deep down I knew I couldn't abandon them. I knew too well what that felt like.

"Let me see them."

Three newborn girls were suddenly placed in my arms and lap. They were magnificent creatures and they all looked like me. I sighed with relief. These girls were so beautiful. How could I not love them?

Hecate approached cautiously. "What would you like to call them?"

I studied each of them and their faces, running my fingers gently over them as they seemed to enjoy my touch.

"Alecto. Megaera. Tisiphone. The Furies."

Primal Scream

I carried for years the internal shrieking
I've learned to ignore
Having numbed the feeling of listening to
Someone cry out in despair
Until my firstborn undid the restraints
For my second-born to unleash that which
was
Fighting to free itself within
I'd been waiting for my entire life
To scream the way I did when
my body released my child
And I am better for it
Finally set free.

__The Furies__

My hips opened up
when I gave birth to them
And with it, everything I had locked there
came rushing out
The pain
The rage
The fury

If I hadn't been conscious
If I hadn't already been trying to heal
I wouldn't have survived that

Many don't.

For the Woman Afraid of Her Body

You've been trusted with a portal
that's far more trouble than you can handle
You are unclean when you bleed
and you're a bitch for being uncomfortable

That's what they've told you

Hands between thighs is an immoral act
Don't you know you are the original sin?
You are to be chaste and completely unsexual

That's what they've told you

Stop.

1.
Purchase a small mirror and place it between
your legs
Draw a map of your valleys, your mountains,
and your rivers
Memorize them

2.
Close your eyes and feel each contour
Squeeze your breasts, know every lump in
them
Measure the distance from your ribcage to
your hips,
Make it a requirement
of anyone you allow in your bed
to accept all measurements as they are

3.
Learn what makes your clitoris throb
Massage it, fantasize, touch yourself
Orgasm loudly
Let every goosebump appear, and curl your
toes
Arch your back
Be beautiful in your moments of ecstasy

4. Your mother's mother's mother gave birth
in her house
Childbirth is not dangerous, it is your special
talent
They put fear in you so that you can hand
your power over
It is not a punishment to have a womb
It is your gift

5. Tell them where it hurts
Cry, bitch, moan;
Scream your head off and name your pain

6. Add to this list as you see fit.
Remove all fear of being born a woman.

A Midwife's Pain

Birth in the time of war is painful
When you know the people you love
Are half target practice
Half warriors for justice
You pray
No one opens fire
On their tender
Delicate.
Fallible skins.
I think as a midwife:
That head could have crowned into my
palms.
I shudder at the thought of those skulls
landing with a thud on hard concrete
Instead of softly resting in my hands.

When watching a baby be born
It brings me to tears
Because I know the world it has arrived into
does not want it alive
Because they are not white
I wonder how my heart can take so much
pain and so much beauty
All at once
I am weeping each time I must release these
bodies.

Sometimes, I want to stop the babies from
being born.
I cry silently, please don't come into this
world.

Please, this is the most alive you might be.
This is the safest you will be. In my hands.
Even at the beginning of your life, they try to
kill you.
They want your momma dead.
In a country where so many of us are cut
open
Born too early. Not enough care.
I beg you

Please. Don't be born.

Please. Be born.
My heart would not be able to take more of
this violence if you were not born.
If I had not witnessed the resiliency of my
people
Still deciding to continue living.
Of Black women still deciding to give birth
And triumphantly succeeding.
One in four are likely to die to bring you here.
I cannot explain the rage that courses through
my body
When I hear another woman hemorrhaged to
death from neglect
When she had a C-section because a doctor
needed to learn
And our bodies are historic sites of
experimentation

I have held laboring women
Their weight on me as I make myself
Strong

To support
To hold
To guide them
As they prepare to release
This body
This life
This Royalty
This burden
Of mothering while Black.

It is a grave situation that
Breaks back and
Breaks hearts
It is too real
The feeling of your heart
Leaping into your throat
Nearly suffocating you

This act of resistance
To still create in the ghastly face of
Death, destruction, execution
Genocide
In fear of this precious cargo
This gift of hope and promise
Being taken too soon from momma's arms
Too soon from dreams coming true
Too soon
Too intentional
Too much history
Repeating
Replay
Replicating itself
If we didn't love these children so much

We might commit infanticide just so
They can leave this planet on our terms

When you tell me to calm down.
Please you don't understand what it's like
To be in the same cycle for over 500 years
To have a baby born into your hands and
write the birth certificate knowing
You might have to read their obituary one
day.

I still remember
That you were created in love in the time of
war
And that you are still as delicate
As you were at that moment of entering.
I have watched your eyes fluttering in your
sleep
As I gently examine your body for the first
time.
And weep
Imagining that one day
Someone else will examine your body for the
last time
Your eyes not fluttering anymore

Not dreaming anymore
A midwife's broken heart
Holding the pain and beauty of millions.

For The Women of Ciudad Juarez

She is opening, slowly
(Poco a poco, m'ija)
At her own steady pace
Sunrise rhythm of dilation,
she loses it during contractions
Gains it when her womb takes a moment
*(No tengas miedo, mi amor. Respira
profundamente)*
Surrounded by a circle of women holding her
Pacing back and forth down the hallway
(Vamos hermana, tú puedes)
Deep guttural moans escape parched lips
As she faces the pain to embrace her child
Experiencing her birth and her
transformation
She is tired and ready
(Todavía falta un poquito)
Prayers sit on our tongues as we sit on our
hands
Watching her blossom
Slowly
Like a rosebud you wouldn't dare force open
(Ya mero vas a conocer tu bebe)

To the Children I've Caught:

To all the children I have had the honor of
being part of their welcoming committee:

The ones I got to know as you grew, making
your mother pregnant with your existence;
You, who preferred the left close to her heart
with your back against her flank, I
contemplate you often.
I struggle to remember each of you uniquely
as the births melt into each other like sunset,
My body feeling the endless hours awake
with your mothers hoping you'd emerge;
Your galloping horse of a heart decelerating
as uterine contractions push your head closer
to the crossover,
Racing once again as the dramatic
metamorphosis unfolds in the most necessary
of pains;
You are otherworldly.
Mother opens the portal releasing this
creature
This intricate wiring of blood vessels,
muscles, hormones, vital organs, bones &
flesh
Still evolving, still becoming something.

I often think, when I prostrate myself before
you, becoming present for your first physical
examination,
What wonder it is that all ten fingers and ten
toes are possible.

That understanding the spiritual science
behind your being makes you indeed magic
For simply manifesting
For becoming.
I am always compelled to be in awe of being
human;
To be this magnificent and expansive while
sobered by my temporary nature.

I am reminded when I can feel your pulse in
your anterior fontanel on the occasion when
I place an arbitrary measure on a
disappearing cervix
That you leave an eternal ocean to
understand the earth and its inhabitants.
The crowning of your head into my hands is
enough to dumbfound me in amazement if
not for my charge;

I remember one hazy late night hour blinking
away sleep as I held a towel, awaiting you,
My jaw dropped watching you
be delivered by your momma
Your body fluidly changing dimensions
spiraling out;
It was seeing you join us for the first time that
reminded me in my weariness
This moment, this day of your birth
Is miraculous, every single breath
Remembering I was one of the first to hear
the symphony of
Your butterfly lungs expanding with air

Marveling at how incredible magical human beings make themselves into this reality

After Birth

You will find yourself
washed ashore with a small body of
your body pressed against yours for survival
they call the place you've woken up in
Motherhood
All the others have found their footing;
Some needed
hip replacements
an infinite stretch of orange pill bottles,
wine bottles and other
delicious medications
an emotional support child
Others figure out how to wear the weight
supported by others or
out of spite

Is there anything else like becoming a mother
that destroys and resurrects you
over and over again?

(I still can't get over how big of a deal they
make about this Jesus cat and that mf never
even gave birth)

Conversation with the River

She told me,
That's the problem with people like us -
The sweet, savory fall on your tongue like
honey folks
The more dulzura y bondad
you have to give
The more they will want.
They will drink you dry, my love.
She advised me,
Protect your deliciousness.
Melt into arms that melt back into you
It is not your duty to quench everyone's
thirst.
Let your rivering love flow into tributaries
Ones that go from lake to lake and find your
ocean again
Raining into your pores and replenishing
your spirit.

Plucked

When my petals were plucked
I mistook my nakedness for triumph;
Not understanding my beauty was nearly
stolen.
A rose is not still
A rose
All spoiled and
Squandered like that.
My body records its unfolding
So well, and has asked for
Protection.
It says: '_If I must lose my blossoms,
let it be to the earth
and not their careless fingers._'
It says: _stop letting
the 'I love you's'
'I love you not's'
Rip me apart._

When I am a bud once more
After the lesson of winter's deep slumber
I remain rooted; a wild flower
Not cut and put into a bouquet
To die
For if they valued me
They would want me
To grow free.

Odiosa

Soy odiosa
That's what I've been told, directly and
indirectly, throughout my life
There's a narrative, a persona that's been
built around how I show up in the world and
how my family has interpreted it
Mainly my mother, because it's her
responsibility to make sure
I act como la gente
But I don't have to hear the word from
anyone else;
just the reaction alone is enough to know
Que yo no soy fácil
That how I express myself is sour and bitter
Rabiosa
Angry
Dicen que no soy simpática ni dulce
Even though I've been forced to be this way

Es mi carácter fuerte que es odioso
Honest and sharp, my words cut even my
own mouth when they come out
They carry rage that I was forced to swallow
for years because we're not allowed to be
angry with our parents.
Never able to protect ourselves from
cocotazos, correas, chancletazos, back slaps
with the aftertaste of blood for daring to
speak
Instead having a suffocating silence forced on
us

Boundaries violated and expected to be docile
and gentle
These are remnants of colonization; traces of
enslaved trauma seasoning the way we
should act
Generations of domestic violence, and the
way that seeped into our mothering and
family dynamics

Punitive love
No one ever truly loves honestly even when
they demand it
No one loves a strong woman when that
strength and will won't bend
Even though the backbone of la patria are
iron-willed women holding it all together

Porque a ella no se le puede decir nada
You can't speak to me in any tone you want
No, you cannot criticize me and make mean
spirited jokes about my body or life
I will not be bullied or told I'm too sensitive
No, I will not shrink to make you feel
comfortable to show up however you want at
my expense
The way you sought to domesticate my
mother
My grandmother
And her mother before her too
This critique is not new
Porque ellas son fuertes
Malcriadas
Rebeldes

Odiosas

Having boundaries looks like a threat to
people who are not used to them
Fiercely loving myself has meant fiercely
protecting the little girl who wasn't and being
the adult woman who will
I was not always this way
Yo era simpática, dique
I don't enjoy being this tough and nearly
impermeable
I don't take joy when my words pierce
I've had to unearth my sweetness and soften
my glare
Smoothing and sanding my rough edges is
constant labor
While never letting my spear go dull or my
shield to be weak
But I would rather die than be silent
Soy odiosa
Sin querer
Pero me defiendo

What Happened to You?

When I look at you, I wonder what was your favorite game when you were 5. I try to figure out whose eyes you have and whose smile you are imitating.

When did your heart get broken? I'm talking about before the romance. I want to know when your childhood dreams were laid to waste.

When did you forget who you are and what happened?
When I look at you, I wonder what you sound like when you laugh recklessly and how chubby your cheeks were when you were one.

I try so hard to remember that we weren't always this
wounded...and if we peel back the layers, there is a well of joy there. What were you like before the innocence was lost?

How did you sit on your mother's hips when you floated in her waters?

Did you stay on her right side because there was more space? Or did you stay to her left so you could be closer to her heart?

How did you press on her bladder or kick
into her lungs?
Did you giggle or hiccup with joy, never
meaning to hurt her but jabbing at her
playfully to remind her you were there?
Do you remember?
Can you imagine?

Demeter, Revisited

I stopped speaking to my mother a long time ago. Yet there was an aching for her in my chest. Much different that the ache I felt when I was raped. An ancient desire between child and their first god, their mother. No matter how much I convinced myself that I could survive without her, I was cutting off my nose to spite my face.

Drowning in forgetfulness, Lethe, and in self-hatred, Styx, I had wailed and lamented, Cocytus, while waddling for far too long in misery, Acheron. I knew these rivers of the Underworld intimately until I found myself in front of the only river I had avoided. Mnemosyne. It ran right in front of his palace.

This is how I came back to life after birth forced me to connect to my muscle memory. Mnemosyne. Memory. The memories that sat behind my pain and rage. It was the most refreshing water I had drank in my whole time coming back to life. I took a deep drink and immediately thought of Demeter.

All I had thought of her was how she hurt and neglected me. But as I remembered her, all the ways that her brothers and sisters treated her came rushing back to me. I knew she slept so much because she did so much to keep the earth alive. Demeter was the reason that humans had food to eat. She was the reason for the living. All the crops harvested were in her name. She sacrificed all she knew how to so that others would stay alive. Including myself.

I wanted her love, I thought angrily, ready to shut myself away from the thought of forgiveness. I drank more deeply and felt myself refreshed from within. I suddenly got a memory of the first time she put me in a dress. My hair was growing untamed in all ways out of my head. She did her best to brush it back and make me look beautiful.

Another sip from Mnemosyne, another flashback flickered in my mind as I watched her toil in the fields alongside the humans and bringing me back my favorite flowers every time, as an apology for her absence. She did her best to let me know that at least she was thinking of me.

At this point, I knelt over the riverbank and was lapping up the water, as if I had never had water before in my life. I remembered the time she let me travel with the forest nymphs to all the places they wanted to show me even though she was scared for my safety. She did her best to make sure I could see the world she never got the chance to explore.

I nearly choked on the water. I had another memory of when I got my period for the first time. She told me it meant that I was a woman. Shortly after, she told all the goddesses that I had my first bleed with stars in her eyes. I was so embarrassed, and she was doing her best to celebrate me in the only way she knew how.

My eyes began to fill with tears. A shadow of the scene when I stood before my mother as she interrogated me about the rumors regarding Adonis. I suddenly heard her voice darken and her mouth twist in rage. *You whore*, she screamed at me, *you disgusting prostitute*! I didn't know better, and I think this was the best she could do to try and warn me about protecting myself from men. That type of love didn't translate though.

The last memories made me burst into tears completely. I saw her memories this time. It was a younger version of my mother. Demeter was in a field alone, sobbing. Her clothes were ripped and she was bleeding. In the distance, I could see my father Zeus buckling his pants with a smug air about him.

Oh, my poor mother. I thought of my daughters and how my mother lived what I lived through.

The next thing I saw was how her brothers and sisters ridiculed her and said awful things about her. Maldita loca estupida. Clown. Ugly bitch. My aunt Hera was the worst of the offenders. I saw her raise her hand to slap Demeter every time she spoke too loudly, stepped out of line or simply was an embarrassment or annoying to her. My mother, with a wide-tooth smile and tears streaming down her face, continued to desperately entertain them and take care of the humans. She did her best to survive.

On my last sip of water, I saw her try for the last time to protect me by telling my father to go check on me when Hades was executing his awful intentions for me. And finally, the image of a parched earth and humans crying out to the sky for mercy came into view. My mother looked crazed and furious, hair wild and her robes dirty and tattered. She was looking for something and had completely neglected anything to do with the crops. I saw her screaming at Helios, the sun.

"Did you see her?! Where is she?!" my mother screamed. The sun directed his rays in the direction of Mount Olympus. I was horrified. *Was my mother looking for me?!*

Her vision changed and I saw Demeter storm into the palace. Hera was pissed and blocked her way.

"Why the fuck do you look like that? GO TAKE A BATH!!" Hera bellowed at her, raising her hand to slap my enraged mother down. My mother caught her hand and shoved her to the ground. My aunt was shocked and all she could do was stare gobsmacked at Demeter marching to the throne room.

Zeus came into her view. He looked disgusted at her appearance sitting on his throne.

"WHERE IS MY DAUGHTER, YOU FUCKING PIECE OF SHIT?!?!?!" My mother screeched. Zeus narrowed his eyes at her.

"And just who the fuck do you think you're talking to like that, maldita loca?" he spat at her.

"WHERE IS MY DAUGHTER?!"

"The humans are dying. Go back to the earth and do your motherfucking job, bitch."

"Are they hungry?! LET THEM FUCKING DIE! IF I DON'T GET MY DAUGHTER BACK, THEY CAN FUCKING BURN."

Zeus stood from his seat. "I let Hades take her. But no one will ever believe her or you, so quit your bitching, you crazy whore."

Demeter's eye's widened before she lunged at my father like a wild animal. He struggled to restrain her as she attempted to claw his eyes out. Zeus looked horrified and immediately, palace guards came to subdue her. She thrashed wildly in their grip, barely containing her rage.

My mother was in rare form. She did her best. All she did was her best. I can release myself now from the pain of not having her the way I wanted her. The least I can do is forgive her.

I looked up from Mnemosyne and focused on the doors of Hades' palace. My own memories hit me in sequential order and like a movie: I saw flashes of Adonis, of Hades and how he slithered his way into my life, and all the moments I thought I would be crazy like my mother too.

There was only one thing left to do. The rage coursing through my body with the realization of how we were set up to be destroyed moved my body with murderous intent.

I stood up and walked through the river, not letting the palace out of my sight as I marched towards it.

It was time to settle the score.

Co-Sign to Violence

Why do we close our mouths at the same
speed we open our bodies and minds to
danger?
Is this not a fire? And were you not taught to
scream and warn me of the flames?
Am I not burning inside for the sins of my
foremothers who never left a warning?

Hoards of women stretch their bones brittle
Stain the inside of their thighs birthing the
blood of their sacrifice
To never reap the fruits of selling their hair
for duty:
Bear them sons, keep her brothers
But who keeps the sisters?

Who warns the girls on the precipice of
puberty about the world that will viciously
steal youthfulness from their step?
We love to see bodies drag themselves in
misery because we need the company
Daughters are left to starve for the wisdom in
the sighs of resignation embedded in between
their mother's words, scoffed at for being
naive

Why have we co-signed to this slow steady
nearly silent massacre of sisters?
What sinister plot have the grandmothers
allowed to be passed through their sons?

We should have never been thrown to the
wolves.
So many of us are fallen favorite earrings
dropped and lost, never to be searched for
Advised to take the blame for man's savage
nature
Asked to wear something blue to accent the
bruises that the white dress brings out in you
Call the rape rough-housing and leave legs
parted for the next bully to finish the job
Enforce a gag rule so there will never be a
shortage of prey for the predators
How often have we let others put a gun to
their heads and play Russian roulette?
Why don't we fight to pull each other from
the edge of loss?

I know we cannot protect people from pain
Some paths must be walked but must we be
so severely misguided and lost?
And I can't look
To watch these countless vessels shucked and
cleaned out of their treasures
We must correct this lest we want to lose our
very existence
For it is the women who will keep birthing it
and it is us who hold up half the sky
We are the most valuable creatures, never the
prodigal daughters
This can't be life without the ones that can
bear it.

The Times I Forgot to Pray (after Kayla Frawley):

1) Playing house,
My stomach always turned
after becoming a wife, so young.

2) When a little white girl and I
played in the sun for hours
her father's hatred of my skin
should have never become my own.

3) The first time I saw my mother on lithium,
I died inside holding the suffocating weight
of what happened after years of too much.

4) When they heard poetry that
passes as normal for a 17-year-old,
no one took the pain seriously.
They were a series of suicide notes
that I was applauded for.

5) When I decided I didn't believe in god
and lost my religion in the search for answers
I wasn't ready for.
I let go of the artificial light to sit alone in my
darkness.

6) The night I tried to kill myself senior year
of high school
I was mad at myself for being afraid of
cutting my wrists
though I started vertically with the wound.

I read off a litany of all the pills I could find
and
waited to wake up dead.

7) That summer afternoon
when I got the news about my father's
betrayal,
I decided instead that if he had failed me
all other men would too.

8) After eight shots of tequila and
sex in an alleyway,
I found my god at the bottom of shot glasses
and bedsheets
trying to fuck the pain of loss away.

9) When the birth control hormones made me
crazy. When the pills made me nauseous
and the Bacardi bottle broke on the floor.
When I took a shard of the glass to my wrist
dropped it, packed my bags, and left my
dorm room.

10) When my grandfather died
I remember his corpse at the funeral home.
There was a moment when all I could do was
cry.
I learned that tears don't have to make sense
with grief.

11) When I finally got my period
and developed into a woman.

I had no clue of the battle these hormones
would start
all I felt was gratitude that I wasn't damaged.

12) That night my heart was ripped out of my
chest.
When I left my body as he entered it,
gripping my wrists,
I stopped fighting and let it happen.
My body betrayed me displaying pleasure
when all I felt was my personal hell.

13) When I could only afford to pay rent and
pretended to fast so my stomach would not
tell the story of poverty to the world;
I didn't know how to ask for help with the
shame I felt, so I starved.

14) When he asked me if I could open my
labia
so he could see the pinks and reds,
capturing it on his camera.
Looking me in the eyes
after we were done,
he said they were hollow and depressed.
I grabbed the money and left as fast
as my nakedness could carry me.

15) When I looked in the toilet
and saw blood.
So much blood; the scent of death
was palpable.
Houses go silent

when something is dying.
It kept dying and
dying and
dying, spilling from between her legs
out into the world.
I did nothing. Paralyzed. Unable to
attend her.

16) When I couldn't get the baby out.
When I had to make the transfers.
I'd get so mad at myself and wonder
what I did wrong.

17) When I hitchhiked in Holland as a 16-
year-old
with all the naiveté and none of the sense
that this was dangerous.

18) When I woke up crying,
my head shook violently and
I was afraid they were going to beat me.
As calmly and quickly as I could
I walked myself to the psych department
told my therapist I was losing it
and spent 8 hours in the crisis room
not knowing.

And in the darkest of moments
prayer did not escape my lips
now I inhale intention and exhale
all the spells and incantations
that make me magic.
I survived like the cat that I am

living so many lives recklessly;
it is time to rest.

Hardened

I was once a gentle babbling brook of a
woman
A butterfly lightness that made my eyes
dance
I flowed quietly, gracefully like innocence
intact
My inner clay, once soft and pliable
Began to dry, crack, and harden
Too much weathering
Suddenly I was the force of hurricanes
I grew into choppy treacherous waters
Difficult
Unforgiving
Dangerous
Hard

She saw me again for the first time, took a
good look, and said,
"Life happened to you."
She said, "What changed your soft light
Replaced it with high beams that blind and
hurt the eyes
Your melodic voice; now full of curses
Sharp and jagged, a switchblade tongue and
glass for teeth?"

What did me in finally
What made me into a fortress of a woman
I've been shaken, rattled to death
A mental break changed me permanently
Too many years of simply surviving

Clawing my way through these tribulations
I am tired, and broken but mending
Seen too much without anyone
understanding
What parts of me I had to give up for
What I've gained
I've become tough as nails
Militant
Demanding
Severe
Imprisoned by steel walls around the
innermost parts of me
I don't bleed so easily now
The sweetness is hard to come by with this
bitter taste
When too many took my delicate world and
roughly
Ransacked me, taking what they wanted

Mourning
Dawns on me when I search for the softness
Finding rockiness and concrete to rest my
head
An icy queen tired of the freeze
If only I could melt
If only I could become spring's first waterfall
and refresh my rivers
Thaw me
Smooth me over
Bring me back to gentle

A Fierce Creature Birthing a Soul

The muscles in the center of her back caved
in, shifting her bones into her new form
Shoulder blades tensing and moving,
begging skin to let them free

Rib bones resembling feathers
Assembling into her wings
I swear she almost bore her teeth and
Assumed her full stature as
Demigoddess
Semidiosa
Not fully human
Not fully divine
Yet required to be both

She must let a new creature nearly
Tear her in half and come back to tell the
story

Her voice, a soft whisper in the wilderness
acquiescing to the pull of the force greater
than her
Might she be Eve,
screaming to the gods for attempting to
punish her?
I think she be Lilith, defiant and poised

Sensual pregnant body that has known God
and lived to tell the story

Her guttural roar will shake the walls of this place and move heaven and earth for a small mighty force.

La Fiera

I grew fangs
My fingers elongated into razor sharp claws
Horns formed where my hairline and
forehead meet, near my temples
Una bestia
Una fiera
Un animal
I would look at my reflection in the muddied
waters and not recognize myself for years

Something awoke in me
Stirring in my head as I pawed at myself
As if I had fleas
There were small creatures
Omalara
The watcher inside me huffed
It was a language I'd know my whole life but
never knew how to speak
Omalara

Children of my body
Body of my flesh and insides
Blood of my blood
Flesh of my flesh
I'd been sleepwalking one thousand years it
seems
Lungs expanding with air and
A deep first cry woke me up
Little girls
And suddenly I was plunged into rawness
A bleeding body, postpartum

Hips twisted like möbius
My mind fractured itself and I walked the
halls of my subconscious
Pacing back and forth, trying to understand
what and why and how
I felt all of my pain and suffering
Both in my body and my heart
Hecate would later tell me that the mortals
called my condition
Depression
Anxiety
Obsessive
Compulsive
Nearly on the edge of psychosis

I wanted to walk into the river with my
children and drown us
This is how I could save them from this world
But it could not be me to rob them of their life
It would have to be me to protect them
I wasn't crazy
I was on other side of motherhood
No longer a girl after knowing so much
But not quite who I was before
Much more fierce and far more deadly

Murdering Hades

"Well, well, well. If it isn't the motherfucker who killed me."

The air choked on itself. The bastard choked on his spit.

The only sound I could hear was the squelching of my wet muddied feet on his linoleum floor and the pounding of his heart. I never broke my glare as I strutted towards the monster of my nightmares, the horror of my heart, and the thorn in my side.

This motherfucker had the audacity to wear white. "Don't try to be an angel now, darling."

I got close enough to see him better. He was an old man now, the dark circles under his eyes showing me the sleepless nights spent torturing others like me were no longer badges of honor.

He stood from his table, perhaps to challenge me, perhaps to keep his wits about him. The closer I got to him, the closer he backed into the corner.

"Don't tell me that Hades is afraid of little old Persephone?"

"I thought you were dead. I made sure of it."

"Ah. What a fucking rookie move. Don't you know that you should never look back? When you murder someone, make sure you aim for the most vital organ, my love."

"I loved you."

"No baby, you loved the idea of me. You loved how I came undone in your hands after you groomed me to do so. You loved the way you melted in my mouth and how I gazed up at you unable to speak. It felt like power to have me on my knees. You loved how I made you feel like a God; you were bold enough to think I was speaking about you when I'd say 'oh my God'."

I was close enough to touch him. Hades stiffened. He seemed horrified that I'd get him dirty.

"Oh? What's this? Are you afraid I will ruin your sparkling white suit with my sullied hands? Would be it awful if someone saw you covered in your own shit? Did you have a date?"

Suddenly finding his boldness, he cleared his throat. "Not that it's any of your business but…"

"Yes, very nice. SHUT THE FUCK UP, VIEJO SUCIO!

You are pestilence. You are worse than anything that has befallen the earth. I hate you deeply and I wish I had never met you in my life!" I screamed, shaking the walls of his hideout, and spitting in his face.

"What's wrong with the motherfucking bane of my existence?", I said scornfully, lifting a clawed muddied finger up to his cheek. Visibly cringing now that I was so close to him, I slowly carved the side of his face with my sharp nails, pressing hard enough to make him think I would draw blood.

"You seem so weak now. I thought you were scary and intimidating when I was a little girl. I thought you were the big bad wolf. El matatan. El mismo fucking demonio. Ay si papi. Que maldito susto pase contigo."

I was confused momentarily at his lack of self-defense. Surely it couldn't be this easy to face my murderer. I looked him in the eyes and felt something in me soften. I wanted to be close to him. To erase the pain of death with pleasure again. To rebuild the fantasy world I grew up in and he had joined. In that softness, he reached out and grabbed me close to his body, forgetting his white suit.

"Why did you come see me Persephone? You can't get enough of me. I can make you feel real good. You know you've missed me."

I was too shocked to immediately respond as the heat of his body warmed the coldness of my skin. I almost forgot why I had come back as his fingers crept up my back looking for a way to disarm (undress) me. He is intoxicating. I closed my eyes as his other hand guided mine to his front, so I could feel how hard he was getting. Hades let go of me and undid his belt. He zipped open his pants and pulled out his cock. My jaw tighten and a wave of rage pulled me out of my shock.

Hades leaned into me again. Close enough to my ear, I could feel his hot breath on my neck. And right then he sealed our fate.

"Good girl. Now get on your knees and show me how much you love me."

The smell of something putrid filled my nostrils as my claws dug in.

I have never heard a man scream the way I did that night. I enjoyed every second of it. He came undone in my hand. His blood spilled over me before I pulled away from him. The sickening sound of flesh ripping was the last thing I heard from him.

"No, my love. Tú eres el demonio? Yo soy la fiera."

Hades' body dropped to the floor as he bled out. His cock was a sad little flaccid appendage in my hand. I had castrated him so many times in my head. I thought I would use a knife to finally take his most prized possession and life in one shot. This was much more satisfying. I waited until he stopped moving, stuffed his cock into his mouth, and put two coins on his eyes.

Hecate waited at the exit for me, smiling. It was time to take the throne.

Purgatorio

I had saved myself so many times. It was the only way to protect my daughters. Losing myself and choosing the men had cost me dearly. The ultimate price was the children, and I would sooner die a thousand deaths before handing mine over so easily.

Omalara. Child of my body. Inhabiting my body was the most revolutionary act I could commit in the world of men. These mighty creatures conceived themselves within me and chose this body, this mind, and this spirit to house them.

I turned this entire world upside down when I took the throne. Souls that had been languishing en el purgatorio were no longer left to their own devices. The harem of wise women whose hearts he had viciously ripped out was rehabilitated. They were, at best, victims of his perverse games and, at the very worst, sexual slaves who died every night longing for even the littlest bit of some semblance of love.

I sat with every single one, one by one, and listened to their stories. The ways in which he lured her into his clutches. Her hand in aiding and abetting him in his conquests. The psychosis the drugs had caused them and the horrible things they did to other women. The forgetting. Oh, the forgetting. She told me everything she had forgotten - how we had been born of the earth when the waters covered the land and we were Gaia and she was us.

We were omolara of this world and have always served as reminders of our primordial origins. Before we walked upright on the earth. Before we expanded our lungs to take in air by inhaling instead of through our skin. Before we grew the ocean within our wombs and kept this going. Before our divinity was stripped of the erotic and became pornographic. Before we had weapons. Before weapons were phallic. Before the phallus was weaponized. Before we became women. Before woman came to mean weak, fragile, and evil. Before Eve.

And when I heard every single last story, I cried with them. And we grieved. We mourned the death of our mothers and foremothers millennia ago. The death of the little boys who fought to be good men and those who turned wicked, we cried bitterly for them too.

And we took accountability without blame. Once the last teardrop dried on the cheeks of all the forsaken, we were finally undrowned. Together we vowed to never let this happen ever again. I know I would make sure of it.

Rain.

The rivers of new-water-old-pain (cleanse
me) cascade from open clouds like hands
welcoming release.

We are let go, let God, let spirit waterfall
between thunder-rumble
Making everything wet with gratitude.

Moon cycle, relentless, needed moon child
like me to wax, become full and resign to the
influences of it all.
I do not know the ending of the story.
I do not pretend to understand the method.

On my way to crone, this transformation
from maiden to women feels chrysalis
cracked soul expanding painfully.

Butterflies find it hard to begin again too with
the agony of death so close to the opening.

I am want.
I am so much want.
I am pleading.
I am not waiting.
I want water.
To shift, form and change me.
To teach me fluidity in a world so rigid.
Thunder shake and rattle my bones; lightning
illuminate chest cavity.
I am ready.

Take old skin and throw it into ocean that
refuses nothing and takes everything I give it.
I am let go.
I am deep let go.
Rain.

Magnolia Soul

A decade ago I asked about dying in the
spring
And when I'd come alive again
The answer was right in front of me
I just didn't know I was looking at it
There's this magnolia tree in front of my
building
I love it when it blooms
This spring her buds were early and the
flowers were about to bloom
A devastatingly bitter cold wilted them
And dead brown blossoms were the
aftermath
Today, a newly warm spring day
I looked up and noticed that there were but a
few yet
Mighty magnolia flowers blooming
Again
I bet there will be green leaves again
The death of coldness being no match for an
invincible
Will to live

My Dark Kingdom

Here in the darkness, I know myself. I claimed my throne and attended to my subjects. I, their Dark Queen and Mother of the Furies. Stronger than Hades and far more powerful.

I didn't want my daughters. They had reminded me too much of the past. But when I saw them and held them, I knew it was up to me to remember what happened to me. They were my joy. They would fuel my fury for retribution.

The scales of justice will be tipped to restore balance to this planet, one in which the Gods have abandoned their post as the moral compass, and the demons have been cultivated and set free to rape and pillage the body of the earth and her inhabitants.

In my ceremonial bath, Hecate sang over me as she scrubbed my body clean. She washed me as though she was trying to remove every trace of him off me. I sobbed the entire time, my body releasing buckets of tears.

"Desahógate m'ija," she whispered as she rubbed my back, my body heaving and shaking. "Undrown yourself."

I held in so much. So much grief. So much pain. My journey to finally dispose of him had taken every last inch of composure to face my death and murder the one responsible for it.

When my body stilled and quieted itself, when my shoulders calmed and the last drop of water left my body, I took a deep breath.

Hecate dressed me in a white silk dress that fit me like a glove. When she was done, she looked at me in the eyes. "Are you ready, my queen?"

I nodded. "It's time to wear your crown. Remember, mi hija, never forget what it took to get here. You will set so many more free." She led me to my throne. I felt something I had not felt in a very long time. Pride. Joy. Light. I took my seat and my crown was placed on my head.

My daughters came from the shadows. The Furies were full-grown and terrifyingly beautiful, like their mother. Nemesis, Circe, The Hours, The Fates, Eris, and my entire royal court knelt at my feet. They rose and waited for me to speak.I motioned to Hecate.

"The rape of Persephone was a wound that echoed through the realms," Hecate began, her eyes gleaming with fury. "But she was not the only one to suffer at the hands of the gods and men. Our sisters, the dark goddesses, stood witness to countless atrocities, each one a dagger to the heart of the natural order."

I stood up from the throne.

"Just and wrathful retribution."

Nemesis stepped forward with a glint of rage in her eyes.

"You will be my right hand. Unleash the rage of all the women and children who have been raped and murdered on Earth." She came up to me and I bowed my head to her before embracing her tightly. Nemesis went back to join everyone else. I spoke again.

"Circe. Hecate's daughter and right hand."

Circe stepped forward. She went to Hecate and hugged her, and immediately began crying. As she calmed down, she came to me. Her voice tinged with bitter resolve, spoke to us. "We may have been banished to the depths of the earth, but we have not forgotten who we are. We are the keepers of ancient wisdom, the guardians of the sacred feminine."

Murmurs of approval came from the crowd as Circe walked back to them. I cleared my throat to speak again.

"Eris!"

From the depths of the shadows, Eris, the goddess of discord, stepped forward. She bowed to me deeply and came up with a sardonic smile playing on her lips. "The gods may have thought to sow chaos among us, but little do they realize that chaos is our domain," she proclaimed, her voice dripping with irony. "Their arrogance will be their downfall."

I smiled as she met my gaze and stepped back. I looked at my daughters and tears welled in my eyes. The Furies stepped forward.

"Avenge the murder of your mother and foremothers. Lay waste to anyone who dared to violate any child or woman in all of existence."

I felt my heart twist in joy and pain. They were my beloved children and a sharp reminder of the horrors many of us have had to survive.

Megaera, my second born spoke. "For every wrong that has been done to you and all women, we will exact a hundredfold vengeance," she intoned, her voice echoing through the darkness like the wailing of lost souls. "Man and god alike will tremble before our wrath."

Finally, Lilith, with her wings unfurled like a dark storm cloud, came forward with a ferocious grace. "I hope you weren't going to go on and have all this fun without me!" she chuckled her voice a thunderous roar that echoed through the cavernous depths. I smiled at her. "Without you Lilith? I wouldn't dare forget your importance to this mission."

Lilith beamed with pride. "Let us harness the primal forces of creation and destruction and unleash them upon our enemies."

The memory of Adonis' death flashed in my mind. I wanted him to know that I didn't hate him. There were some men who deserved redemption, and I prayed for him.

"Someone get me Prometheus. A man who was willing to risk his liver to steal fire from condescending Gods is someone I want to speak to."

Circe spoke up.

"My Queen, we will empty half the Earth."

"So be it. There is no other punishment for their heinous crimes but death."

I turned to sit down and draw up the list of criminals that needed to be sought out but stopped. My warriors looked at me.

"Mount Olympus is last. When you storm the palace, make sure to come and get me. Drag Poseidon up there too. Make sure Zeus is in the same room. I want to personally rip them apart the same way I killed their brother."

Hecate stifled a laugh.

"My Dark Queen, you have done enough."

I smirked.

"Oh, I know. This one is for Medusa and my mother."

To My Former Self Ten Years After Her First Mental Breakdown
September 2022

You did the best you could with what you had endured. We were deeply mentally ill for the better part of our twenties, and it wasn't your fault.

J. Warren told you when he caught your collapsing sanity in his hands. You needed a break. You'd been trying to carry your broken pieces alone, running for your life. I love you so much. You ran and you fought for our life with all you had. No one should ever go through what you went through.

That breakdown was 27 years in the making. His raping you viciously and your upbringing collided that summer when you were pursuing your deepest and most precious dream.

I love how you plunged into the depths of your abyss and held onto our inner little girl's dreams. You excavated our wish to be a doctor and became the original medicine woman - a midwife. You did that baby. No one else but you held on fiercely through turbulence and pain to our inner little girl. And for that, I am grateful to you.

How miraculous that you immediately turned to birth work after you were murdered and discarded. It would be midwifery and becoming a mother that would ultimately save your life. It would be the hands and hearts of other women that would wash your pain and suffering away. You would break down at the beginning of a nurse-midwifery program that was never your way into this work. You trusted yourself to bring us where we are going. I believe you are one of the most noble people in this world. Look at you - healing so that you may be a conduit for the healing of so many. You're a miracle.

You were so scared and so alone. And in that darkness, you were brave. A light to my current life and to so many others. You are beautiful. Thank you for fighting to stay alive. Thank you for your relentless pursuit to heal and be whole. Future us is incredibly grateful that you set us up to live a life you doubted you'd stay alive long enough to see. I love you. I forgive you. I am so proud of you.

I love you. I love all of us. Carmencita. Ynanna. Carmen.

Printed in the USA
CPSIA information can be obtained
at www.ICGtesting.com
LVHW040129210624
783567LV00002B/79